Other People's Butterflies

CORA RUSKIN

Art Over Chaos - artoverchaos.com
ISBN: 978-1-7359375-2-6
First Edition: June 2021

FOR DEBBIE

creep

chapter one

The girls' hockey team cascades down the steps and I scoot sideways to avoid being trampled. There is a roar of noise – chatter and laughter and trainers slapping the concrete and hockey sticks clacking against each other – which gradually subsides as the Birchwood Bitches make their way onto the playing field. That's not their official team name, it's just what every other hockey team in the county calls them. I stand up, adjust my skirt and take a good, long drag of summer air. Then I bounce up the steps and go inside, feeling the adrenaline kick in.

The changing room is empty, apart from all the bags. We don't have lockers so the bags just sit on the benches, completely unguarded. I head towards the back of the room, just in case someone comes in. It wouldn't be a big deal if someone did. There are toilets at the back of the changing room – I could pretend I was on my way there.

I perch on a bench, itching with anticipation. Next to me is a pile of neatly folded clothes, and next to the pile of neatly folded clothes is a pink, fake snakeskin bag. When I was new at this, and nervous and unsure and getting regular jolts of sickly guilt, I used to poke and prod other people's bags like they were presents under the tree on Christmas Eve. I would pat the outer pockets, trying to figure out the ambiguous shapes inside them, afraid to do any unzipping. Now, I have basically no morals so I just dive straight in like I own everything.

I rummage through the bag, pushing aside a student handbook, tube of lip gloss, pencil case, etc. until I find the phone. Luckily, it's one of the 50 percent of phones in this school that isn't password protected. Not that it would necessarily matter if it was – I have a few tricks for hacking into phones – but it's always great to find one just sitting there unprotected, like a gift.

Sometimes it's fun to try and work out whose phone it is by looking through the messages, but today I go straight for the photos. The first few are selfies, so that's that mystery solved. Melanie Kingston stares back at me, raising a nicely-plucked eyebrow in a "Go on, I dare you" expression. I skim past the selfies, a few soppy pictures of her and a dude I don't recognise kissing each other's faces, a pair of red shoes, a fancy dessert–

EW EW EW dick pic EW! I swipe through a few more fleshy snaps until a splash of colour stops me.

Well, well. Melanie Kingston has a tattoo. A lower-back butterfly tattoo to be exact, which ought to look trashy and clichéd but somehow it looks ... real. Its wings are a rich coppery colour with black edges. You can even see the little bobbles on the ends of its antennae, and it has a delicate shadow as if it's lifting its wings just above Melanie's skin. I send the picture to my phone, along with one of the soppy face-kissing photos because I want to find out who the guy is.

I move on to the next phone. And the next. And the next. I cherry-pick the bits of information I want, typing up occasional notes on my own phone.

• Judging by a handful of recent, covertly taken photos, Misha Hawthorn has a bit of a thing for Mr. Rodríguez (Why? Possibly the Spanish accent).
• Grace Bagshaw and Aoife McCall have had a falling-out, due to Aoife being insensitive about Grace's sister's eating disorder (Aoife is insisting people with anorexia don't eat Nutella straight out of the jar).
• There appears to be a romance blossoming between Holly Douglas and a boy named Crash who is always horny and cannot spell (He thinks "kinky" is spelled "kincky").

After about fifteen minutes of this, I leave the changing room with my haul of info and the kind of buzz that's difficult to get without doing anything illegal.

So, clearly I'm not a very nice person. No, actually, I'm nice enough. I'm friendly, and I say "please" and "thank you" and I smile a lot. I'm still nice; I'm just not good anymore. I don't think there's much point in being good when you're on your own. You need someone to be good to. When I was sixteen, for example, I had people to be good to.

before the beginning

Right, then. I'm sixteen. It's the summer after GCSEs and it's one of those evenings where the air outside feels like a warm bath. Like something posh women would pay for at a spa. I've got my bedroom window open and the sweet reek of hay drifts through from the fields as I try to get my hair looking right.

I'm not that pretty, so I have decided to be blonde instead. A bright, sunny blonde, with candy-coloured hair accessories. Sometimes I even wear it in bunches, like a primary school kid. People refer to me as "bubbly" which I guess is fair enough. I feel bubbly sometimes, like a bottle of Coke that's been shaken up.

My face looks the same as it ever did: green eyes, fair skin, and a nose that I don't get along with. I'm 5'4" now, not particularly skinny or particularly chubby. I have good tits, apparently (Craig Underhill said they were good and he's, like, a connoisseur of tits), but my arse is as flat as two pancakes. Not even those fluffy, American-style pancakes. The completely flat kind.

"Gwen!" Mum's voice barrels up the stairs.

"What?!"

"Don't forget to feed the hens before you go out!"

"I never forget!" I shout this in a slightly wounded voice, though the only reason I never forget to feed the hens is because she never forgets to remind me.

My hair is as good as it's going to get and I can do my make-up on the bus, so I grab my handbag and dash down the stairs. As I'm heading out into the garden, Dad is heading back in. He does that stupid thing where he pretends to be the paparazzi, taking photos of me. I'm in a good mood so I play along, striking cheesy poses.

"So tell us a leetle about zis marvellous outfit you are wearing zis evening?" he says, holding out a pretend microphone and speaking in a camp, French accent.

"Well, the dress is Primarni. And the wellies are tastefully adorned with mud and chicken shit."

"Ahem, chicken what?"

"Chicken poo," I say, rolling my eyes because the swear jar was Mum's idea and Dad is only pretending to be on board with it.

All the playfulness drains out of Dad's voice as he says "I saw that fox again. The one with the dark belly."

"How close was it?"

"About halfway across the field. If it gets any closer, I'm shooting it."

As I head towards the shed, I wonder if he would actually shoot it. Dad's never shot a thing that could've lived, but he's really got it in for this fox. He reckons it's after our hens.

The air inside the shed is stifling, but it has that comforting, white spirit and sawdust smell that reminds me of Sunday afternoons spent hiding out here with Ethan, eating pick 'n' mix and reading comics.

It's a wonder Mum and Dad used to let us play inside the shed, what with all the lethal-looking tools hanging from the walls. At least Dad used to lock up the air rifle back then. Now, he just leaves it on the bench unless he's taking it out to the fields for target practice (empty beer cans and baked bean tins). I go along with him sometimes, and so did my brother Darren before he left for university. I'm a decent shot.

I scoop a cup of chicken feed from the bag and bring it out of the shed. The hens are already rushing towards me, and when I scatter the feed they go berserk. They are white-feathered Sussex hens, and their names are Marjory, Helen, Susie, and June. When we first got them as tiny, fuzzy chicks, Dad kept threatening to eat them as soon as they were big enough. He said we should name them Stew, Pie, Casserole, and Roast Dinner. So I named them after his mum and aunties, and now I'm pretty sure they are safe from the pot, even if they stop laying.

Wellies off. Strappy sandals on. I never wear heels – it's a long walk to the bus stop at the edge of the village. Everything is a long walk when you live in the arse end of nowhere, which I do. Swanmeer is quiet and green and boring. There's nothing at all to do unless you can afford riding lessons, which I can't.

The bus trundles along narrow roads lined with overgrown hedges until it gets to Wootley. This is where Martine and Angie get on, and I wave at them frantically from the back of the bus.

It's weird to see Angie wearing a dress. This summer, she's mostly worn shorts and t-shirts and this tatty denim waistcoat with loads of pockets for keeping sweets and condoms in. She's the type of girl my mum calls "brassy". Martine, as always, looks stunning but seems completely unaware of this. Her parents are from Mauritius, and when she wears fake flowers in her hair and smiles shyly, she looks like something from a tourist brochure designed to convince middle-aged white guys to spend crazy money on an exotic holiday.

"Have you got them?" says Angie, plopping down beside me. Her breath smells boozy – she and Martine must've been pre-drinking.

"Yep." I fish the three fake driving licenses out of my handbag. "They weren't that difficult to make, actually. Maybe I should start a business."

By the time we get into town, Martine is nervous and Angie has applied five layers of mascara in a misguided attempt to look sophisticated. Crap, I thought the fake IDs would be the difficult part and then it'd be plain sailing.

In the twilight, Club Ruby is all lit up and enticing, with a heavy-set bouncer at either side of the door. Okay then, I am not a sixteen-year-old with a fake ID. I am an eighteen-year-old with a university place, a car, and a discreet tattoo. I can hold my drink and have nothing to prove.

Straightening my spine, I swagger up to the door of the club, wondering if I should flirt with the bouncers. Ten seconds later, all three of us are inside. Well, that was disappointingly easy.

Martine has a fit of nervous giggles as soon as we're out of earshot of the bouncer, so I offer to buy her a drink to calm her down, and head for the bar. Club Ruby isn't exactly what I expected. It looks properly glamorous from the outside, but inside the soft red lighting makes it look like one of the brothels you see on crime dramas. Also, it stinks a bit. I'm not sure what it stinks of, exactly – maybe a combination of booze and sweat?

There aren't that many people in the club, but almost everyone is clustered around the bar. While I wait to be served, I look back at Martine and Angie, who have claimed a little booth next to the dancefloor. Martine has stopped giggling now and Angie is stroking her arm soothingly. It's easy to feel protective towards Martine, she is that kind of girl. She'll always have someone looking out for her.

A man brushes past me. As he does so, he puts his hand briefly, casually, on my lower back. It doesn't bother me, and the fact that it doesn't bother me gives me a little buzz. It feels like a victory. I'm smiling triumphantly as I order the drinks.

By the time I get back to Angie and Martine, they've both picked out targets for the evening. Angie, after much deliberation, has settled on a broad-shouldered gym bunny in a vest, and Martine has her eye on a taller, paler specimen with very tight jeans and an angular face.

"So, who do you like?" Angie asks.

Ah, shit. I wish she wouldn't ask me that. It always takes me back to being thirteen, having to pick out a love interest from a row of almost identical boy band members. It was a bloody minefield. You can't just pick the one everyone likes (even thirteen-year-olds know that sexual jealousy is a thing to be avoided if at all possible) but you have to be careful not to pick the "wrong" one. The one with the big nose, or eyes that are too close together, or hair that just looks like normal hair instead of a carefully-sculpted creation. It was supposed to be easy, because you were supposed to feel something. Butterflies in the stomach.

I scan the room, scrutinising the men and trying to decide who is objectively the most attractive. My gaze snags on a bloke in a *Detective Gecko* t-shirt.

Detective Gecko is like the best web comic in the world, ever. It's about a private detective who happens to be a gecko (kind of a Ronseal title – it does what it says on the tin) and it's dark and surreal and hilarious.

"I like that guy," I say, pointing.

"He's about thirty," says Angie, appalled. "He's not even that good-looking, why do you like him?"

"I like his t-shirt."

"It does show off his arms nicely," Martine points out, and I belatedly notice that *Detective Gecko* man has pretty sizable biceps. I take a sip of my drink, which is bright purple and looks better than it tastes, and say nothing. I really can't be arsed to explain myself, and why the thought of fangirling about web comics with this guy seems way more appealing than touching his muscly arms.

An hour later, I'm dancing with *Detective Gecko* man. With a couple of purple drinks inside me, I shimmied over to him on the dancefloor, pointed at his t-shirt and gave him a thumbs up. Voilà – instant connection. Like something from a romantic movie, except we are not dancing very romantically. He dances like a dad – like my dad, in fact – and I follow his lead, just throwing my limbs around and generally going bananas. It's actually really fun. When I catch a glimpse of Martine and Angie, they are grinning encouragingly. Angie now seems less concerned that the guy is twice my age and is making indelicate suggestions via the underappreciated art of mime. I stick my tongue out at them and continue dancing like a gibbon on speed.

Another hour later, I am holding Angie's hair back in the graffiti-covered toilets while Martine fights to control her sympathetic gag reflex. Hopefully we'll get better at clubbing with practice. Angie gave it a go with the gym bunny, grabbing his arm as he moved past her at the edge of the dance floor. He paused and looked at her for half a second, then made a vague "I'm going somewhere else to hang out with other people" gesture and slipped away. Martine had no more luck with the man in the tight jeans, who spent most of the evening flirting enthusiastically with the barman.

"Did you get that guy's number?" Martine asks me, while Angie continues retching.

"Nah, he's too old for me. We were just having a laugh."

Martine smiles a slow smile and puts a hand on the side of my face. "You're a very … free spirit," she says, slurring a little. Martine is such a lightweight. She's drunk half the amount me and Angie have drunk, and she's totally wasted. At least she's not a puker.

Angie, done with throwing up, rests her head on the toilet seat and says, "I love you guys."

"I love you too," I say, in unison with Martine, and maybe it's the alcohol but I 100 percent mean it. I love these girls. I want to wrap them in a big, fluffy blanket of love and keep them safe forever.

the actual beginning

chapter two

Ah, sweet sixteen. Some moments are almost dangerously sweet, though. It's like a Krispy Kreme donut. Delicious when you eat it, but about a minute after it's gone you've got this weird aftertaste in your mouth, like the absence of sugar tastes awful.

This is where everything goes sour. I'm seventeen, and in the lower sixth form. It's a Saturday afternoon in February, and February-type things are happening. Mucky weather. Snowdrops and crocuses springing up all over the place. Easter eggs in the shops. The only unusual thing that's happened is that Hayley Coldridge has invited me to hang out at her house with Jess MacPherson, Tony Parker and Big Jimmy.

This is highly suspicious for two reasons. Firstly, because she hardly speaks to me at school. None of them do, actually. I mean, Jess and I sat next to each other in

Maths last year because Mrs. Waverly loves her seating plans; and Big Jimmy is in my Geography class and sometimes says hi, or catches my eye and looks exasperated when Mr. Broderick makes a particularly bad pun. But that's it, really. It's also suspicious because Hayley hasn't invited Martine or Angie. None of us ever get invited to stuff that the other two aren't invited to, so this is strange and intriguing.

I take the bus into Birchwood – Hayley lives about a three minute walk away from school. I walk up her neat gravel drive and ring the doorbell, feeling unsure of myself. The feeling doesn't go away when she opens the door and beams at me with her naturally perfect teeth (she never even had braces) and her big, blue, Bambi eyes.

"Hey you, come on in. Everyone's watching Netflix in the den."

Ooh, I think this is one of those houses where you can watch Netflix shows legally. I follow Hayley through the hall and down a short flight of stairs, into a room where Jess, Tony, and Big Jimmy are sprawled across cream leather sofas, watching a massive telly. There's a chorus of hellos, though Tony seems pretty engrossed in the show and Jess doesn't look up from her phone. Big Jimmy smiles his lopsided smile at me and swings his long legs sideways to make room for me on the smaller of the two sofas. There's plenty of room for Hayley on the other one, but she opts to sit on Tony's lap instead, thus blocking his view of the telly and commanding all of his attention. Hayley doesn't mess about.

For a while, nothing really happens. We watch *Stranger Things.* Jess is glued to her phone the whole time. I chat a bit with Hayley, who shifts about on Tony's lap in a way that must be making him uncomfortable. I make sure to say nice stuff about Martine, because she's had a starry-eyed crush on Big Jimmy for about two years. I keep shooting little glances at him, trying to figure out if he's taking any of it in.

Jess leaves the room, probably to charge her phone. Then Hayley says she's going to get snacks and leaves too, dragging Tony behind her. Now it's just me and Big Jimmy in the den, and I realise with mounting discomfort that his arm is resting behind me on the back of the sofa. Is that a move? Maybe his arm's just tired. I turn to look at him, hoping I can read his intentions on his face. As I turn, a straggly bit of hair falls across my face. Big Jimmy reaches out and tucks it behind my ear.

Okay, that was definitely a move. I shake my head so that the lock of hair falls again, to show him that I don't appreciate him tidying me up. I'd probably be more convincing if I weren't grinning, but I can't help it – it's some kind of nervous reaction. He grins back and tucks the hair behind my ear again, and I shake it free again. Now I'm grinning because I'm actually kind of enjoying this. It feels like a game, and it feels like I'm winning somehow.

We carry on. Tuck and shake, tuck and shake. I think he's going to kiss me. If he does, I'm going to kiss him back.

I don't particularly want to, but I have to kiss somebody sometime and I may as well get it over with. I'm assuming the desire to kiss will kick in once I'm actually doing it. Like in a romantic comedy, when one character kisses another out of the blue. Maybe they're arguing, or waiting for a train, and the mood isn't noticeably romantic but then the guy kisses the girl and there's a little bit of music. Sparkly sounding, with the notes rising upwards, and you can almost feel it in your stomach. Tingly.

His hand cups the side of my face, I close my eyes automatically, and then it's happening. Our mouths slide slickly over each other, like our lips are coated in oil or something. Romantic comedies have lied to me – kissing does not feel like the music sounds. Maybe the music is only there to cover up the embarrassing squishing noises coming from between two faces. Now Jimmy's tongue is in my mouth and I don't like it; it's all slimy, like a fat slug. I pull away and there is a horrible what now? moment. He stares at me, red-lipped and confused, and says, "You okay?"

"Yeah," I say, in a bright voice. I wipe his spit off my mouth and jump up off the sofa. "I'm gonna get a drink, do you want anything?"

"No thanks, I'm good."

I'm dashing up the stairs before he has a chance to say anything else. My heart is pounding, but I don't think it's pounding in the way it's supposed to.

In the kitchen, Hayley is pouring a big bag of tortilla

chips into a mixing bowl, and Tony is sitting at the kitchen table, watching her with a hungry look on his face. When he sees me hovering in the doorway, he gives me a sly smile and says, "So how are things going with BJ?"

"Okay," I say, and my voice comes out all high-pitched and panicky.

"Did he put the moves on you yet?"

"We kissed."

There you go, Tony and Hayley. Proof that Gwen Foster is a normal, red-blooded woman with normal, red-blooded woman feelings. Spread the word.

"Yay! That's awesome," says Hayley, clapping her hands together in glee. "So how was it?"

"Um ... good," I say, because how the hell am I supposed to respond to that? 'It felt gross and intrusive and I can't imagine ever getting used to it?'

"So are you gonna go out with him?"

Woah, wait, what? I'm supposed to go out with him now? No way. I really don't fancy kissing him again, and besides, if anyone's going out with Big Jimmy it's going to be Martine.

"Nah, I don't think so."

"Why not?" says Hayley, frowning. "What's wrong with him?"

"Nothing, I just ... I'm too busy for a relationship at the moment."

Tony coughs, and the cough sounds an awful lot like the word "bullshit".

"But that's the whole reason I invited you over!" Hayley exclaims. "Jimmy's liked you for ages."

Shit shit shit, this is a total mess. I have to go and talk to him and convince him not to like me, and to like Martine instead. But what if he tries to kiss me again?

"You could at least give him a chance," Hayley continues, pouting like a sulky kid.

"He's actually a really good guy," Tony adds.

My head is spinning. I can't go out with Big Jimmy. Martine will hate me and I'll hate it and I feel a little queasy and my mouth doesn't feel right. It's like I've just been to the dentist.

"Yeah, well, I'm not good, so we'd be a bad match," I say, and I walk out of the kitchen, down the hall, and out the front door. It's raining.

the break-up

chapter three

It's Monday morning, and I've been in a bad mood all weekend. I'm starting to wonder if I was actually telling the truth to Hayley and Tony about me not being a good person. Maybe I'm a total bitch who leads boys on by teasing them and kissing them, then rejects and humiliates them. Maybe I'm like the bitchy cheerleader in American high school movies, which sucks because I never thought of myself that way. I always wanted to be the sassy best friend who's actually way more interesting than the lead and gets all the funniest lines.

I wasn't planning on telling Angie or Martine what happened, but by the time the bell rings for morning break, I feel like I have to tell them something. I'll give them a censored version of events (they don't have to know that I kissed Big Jimmy, just that I kissed someone) and get some reassurance that I'm not a total cow for refusing to go out with him. I know I can count on them for this. Angie is loyal to a fault, and if I told her I'd murdered someone she'd assume that the murder victim totally deserved it and would probably offer to be a character witness in my trial. Martine is a pro at seeing the best in people, so if I told her I'd strangled someone with a garden hose then dissolved the body in acid, she'd say something like "Well, you may be a murderer but at least you tidied up after yourself."

During morning break, the three of us usually hang out in this cosy little nook under the stairs that lead up to the science rooms. There's not much foot traffic, so it's relatively quiet and you can have a private conversation without people listening in. By the time I get there, Angie and Martine are sitting with their heads close together, looking at something on Angie's phone.

Getting straight to the point, I drop down beside them and ask "Am I a total bitch?" Both their heads snap up, and Angie hesitates for a second before saying "Yes." At first I think she's just winding me up, but then I see the looks on her and Martine's faces. Angie's mouth is firmly set in a grim, straight line. Martine looks flustered and upset.

"What's going on?" I ask, getting this sick, sinking feeling like the floor isn't totally solid anymore.

Angie looks down at her phone and reads aloud "Why is your mate Gwen such a stuck-up prick tease? She was totally leading Jimmy on, kissing him and stuff. Now she won't even give him a chance even though he's been crazy over her for ages." She rushes over the last few words, presumably for Martine's benefit, then looks up and gives me an accusatory stare. "So you've been getting off with the guy your best friend has liked forever and a day?"

"It was one kiss," I say, directing this at Martine. "It wasn't even any good, he uses too much tongue."

"Oh, well, thank you," says Martine, looking at me directly for the first time and lacing her voice with rare, potent sarcasm. "Very good of you to jump on that grenade for me."

"Look, I didn't plan it. It just happened."

"Did he force you?" says Angie.

"No."

"Then it shouldn't have just happened. You should've stopped him."

Now I'm angry, because none of this makes any sense. "Why? Why the hell shouldn't I kiss him? He's not Martine's boyfriend, she doesn't own him. Have I contaminated him or something?"

"Okay, you have to be doing this on purpose, because nobody's that dense," says Angie, and my fists are actually clenching.

Martine huffs out a short, irritated sigh, and says, "I think she genuinely doesn't get it."

"Let me explain then," says Angie. "You've totally stabbed Martine in the back. For literally years you act like you're not even interested in boys, then you take the first opportunity to get off with the one she really likes. Are you even attracted to him?"

Saying no will make the situation worse, I'm sure of it. But I don't fucking care. "No, I'm not."

"Why would you go around kissing people you're not attracted to?" says Angie, looking incredulous. "Is it some kind of power play? I can't believe I'm saying this, but you're kind of a slut."

I get up on my knees to give myself a height advantage, and stare into Angie's reddening face. "Are you fucking kidding me? *You're* calling me a slut?"

"I only get with boys I actually *like.* Boys I actually *feel* something for."

"Then I guess you must feel something for half the boys in this school," I spit. I've gone into puffer fish mode – poisonous spines sticking out all over the place. I bite my lip, trying to calm down because this is getting out of control. But then Martine says something unforgivable.

I look at her, and she doesn't look upset or angry anymore. There's confusion on her face, and maybe a tiny, sickening trace of pity. "I just don't understand what's wrong with you," she says, shaking her head like I'm a frustrating crossword puzzle. "Most of the time you're a really good person, but every so often it's like there's something … broken, or missing."

It feels like being punched in the gut. I thought I'd done such a good job of hiding the part of me that doesn't work properly, but apparently not. I stand up, tell them both to go fuck themselves, and walk away.

lana the spy

chapter four

It has been three weeks. Martine and Angie aren't speaking to me, and I'm not speaking to them. I think we're properly broken up. This is crazy. What about all that friends forever stuff? What about all those things Angie posts on social media about how we're going to be crazy old ladies together, causing trouble in the nursing home? What about the friendship bracelet Martine made me in Year 9? What about all those Beyoncé songs? Is everything horseshit?!

For the first couple of days, I was so angry (mostly with them but also with myself, a little bit, I think) that I didn't want to talk to anyone. I ate lunch by myself without even noticing I was by myself. When I finally cooled down, I realised I ought to make some new close friends to hang out with, mostly so Martine and Angie didn't see me all alone and pathetic. So I started hanging around the edges of other friendship groups, making the effort to talk to everyone.

Here's the thing about opening yourself up to human connection and new friendships: It fucking sucks. Old friendships are easy and comfortable. They're made of love and in-jokes and shared experiences. They don't have to be perfect and you don't have to be perfect when you're in them. New friendships are awkward and clumsy and unsatisfying. After a couple of weeks of stilted conversations about things I really don't care about, I realised that as much as I hated Martine and Angie, I hated everyone who wasn't Martine and Angie even more.

So now it's a Saturday afternoon and I'm alone in my room, feeling like crap on a cracker. I actually kind of wish Darren was home from uni. Arguing with him would give me something to think about, at least, but he won't be back until the summer. I have nothing to do (well, I have some homework but you know what I mean – I have nothing I actually want to do) so I go on Facebook.

Facebook is one of those things that ought to make you feel better about life. Instagram has too many people showing off their unobtainable abs, and Twitter is for arguing with strangers, but Facebook has a cosiness about it. People's mums and nans are on it. It's full of pictures of cakes and beaches, and people talking about the cute stuff their cat does. Also, it tells you that you have a bazillion friends. Well, 117 in my case. But that's where it all falls apart, because how can I have 117 friends and no-one to hang out with? I scroll gloomily through my list of friends and come to the conclusion that most of them are little more than strangers. I throw my phone on the bed. Whatever, I don't need friends – I will go out and have fun on my own.

I decide to see a movie. It doesn't matter if there's nothing good playing; I just want to be at the cinema. I want buttery popcorn and a Slush Puppie. I want that familiar buzz of excitement as the lights go down. I want that strange feeling at the end of a movie, when you emerge from the darkness with a crowd of other people and it's like waking up from a collective dream. A weird kind of intimacy.

On the bus into town, I check cinema listings on my phone and find myself going back and forth between a romantic comedy called *The Guy Upstairs* (which is "heart-melting" apparently), an animated film called *Fish Out of Water* ("heart-warming") and a 1940s-set spy movie called *Dead Tulips* ("thrilling"). The spy movie wins eventually, because I don't feel like having my heart melted or even warmed today, but I am always in the mood to be thrilled.

Queuing for a ticket, the couple in front of me start making out and I try not to think about Big Jimmy and his big, slimy tongue. I feel suddenly self-conscious. I can't see anyone else here on their own – it's all couples and little groups and parents with kids. Maybe I look like a loser.

Still, it's dark in the cinema and everyone stares straight ahead at the screen, so it's unlikely anyone will notice my friendless state. I feel better as I nestle into my seat, munch a fistful of popcorn and watch the adverts. Anticipation flutters pleasantly in my stomach.

Two hours later, I have a new favourite movie. I also have a new favourite character and her name is Lana Barrington. She's a badass double agent (or possibly a triple agent or a double reverse quadruple agent – the plot of *Dead Tulips* is pretty confusing) who's so devious that her own dad nicknames her "Poison Candy". She's very femme fatale-ish, with black hair and blood-red lips. She wears this pearl necklace, and one of the pearls is full of cyanide in case she ever finds herself in a jam. In the movie she gets into, like, seventeen jams, but she never bites down on the cyanide pearl because she always finds a way to wiggle out of it. She also has a little black book, which looks empty because she writes in invisible ink, and she keeps information about everyone she meets in it.

I didn't get the point of the little black book at first, because she wasn't writing down state secrets or anything – it was all stuff like which cocktail waitress a married man flirts with at a bar, or who's been pawning their grandmother's jewelery. Gossipy stuff. But then there's a scene where a guy asks her about it and she says "Information is currency. And I mean to be very rich."

By the time I leave the cinema, it's dark and the air is biting cold. My breath swirls around my face like smoke.

On my way to the bus stop I nip into Superdrug and buy a packet of black hair dye and a deep red lipstick called "Kiss of Death".

possibly pregnant

On Monday morning, I colour my lips with the Kiss of Death lipstick and examine my reflection in my bedroom mirror. I think I look pretty good with black hair, though Mum says it washes me out. I'm hoping the red lipstick doesn't get any stink eye from teachers like Mrs. Clearwater, who are overzealous when it comes to enforcing the school's dress code. Sixth form girls are allowed to wear make-up, but it has to be "workplace appropriate" make-up. No glitter, no goth stuff, no crazy colour combinations. It doesn't make sense to me. Supposedly they're getting us used to workplace dress codes, but what if we end up working as children's entertainers or bar staff in a goth nightclub?

I feel different. I feel like a snake that's shed its skin – all new and shiny and venomous.

My first class of the day is Spanish. I get there nice and early, sit at my desk and watch everyone else pour into the classroom. Matt Richardson, propping up his pointy, ugly guitar against the wall. Sheba Jones, wearing her boyfriend's hoodie again. Kelly Kowalski, who stares at me and says, "Dude, why did you dye your hair?"

I smile my new, blood-red smile and say "I just felt like a change."

Maybe I ought to feel self-conscious, but I don't. My attention is elsewhere, focussed on all the other kids in the class as they take their seats, chatting and scraping their chairs across the floor and raising a hubbub of noise that makes it impossible to hear distinct conversations. I think of Lana Barrington. "Information is currency. And I mean to be very rich." If I could crack open the heads of everyone in this classroom, like eggs, what kind of secrets would come pouring out?

This (admittedly gruesome) mental image lingers at the back of my mind. At morning break, I go to the toilets to pee and reapply lipstick. As I stand in front of a dingy square of mirror above an ancient, once-white sink, I hear someone in one of the cubicles puking. The retching sound is so sudden and violent that it makes me jump, and I draw a red line halfway across my cheek.

As I'm fixing this little slip-up, Petra Rawlins emerges from the cubicle. Her face is the colour of maggots. "You okay?" I say, automatically.

"Yeah," she says, sounding drained.

Petra and I aren't really friends, except in a social media way. I've not had anything approaching a conversation with her in months, and now doesn't seem the time to start. Instead, I glance at her while she's splashing her face with water, hoping she hasn't got anything contagious.

As I look at her, a few details of Petra's appearance seem to detach themselves from the general picture. Her pasty face. Her scraped-back hair, like she knew there was a good chance she'd end up puking today and wanted a hairstyle suitable for leaning over a toilet bowl. Her worried expression. Her uncharacteristically baggy top. Holy crap, is Petra pregnant?

She leaves the toilets while I'm still fixing my lippy, moving like she's walking on broken glass. Pregnant or not, I feel a sudden urge to just walk up to her and hug her and tell her everything's going to be okay. But I squash the impulse like a bug.

I need more information. At lunchtime, I wolf down my pizza and salad and head straight to the computer room. My data plan is pretty stingy, so I often use the school computers instead of my phone. I log onto Facebook and examine Petra's profile, looking for clues. Her relationship status is set to single. I look through the photos for signs of a potential baby daddy, but can't find any. And Petra doesn't seem like the kind of girl to get knocked up by a stranger. It just doesn't add up.

The door of the computer room swings open and I look up to see Petra walking in. I get ready to close the browser window if she comes anywhere near me, but she doesn't. She sits at a computer in the row opposite, and starts talking to the girl sat next to her, who turns out to be Emily Holbrook. She's in my tutor group, and so short I couldn't see her behind her computer.

"How are you feeling?"

"Better, but not a 100 percent."

"Did you throw up?"

"Yeah, at morning break. But then I started feeling better."

As a note of embarrassment creeps into Petra's voice, it occurs to me that unlike Emily, I'm not short enough to be invisible behind my computer. I reach into my bag and pull out my headphones, then plug them into the computer and pop the buds in my ears. There you go Petra, the only person who could overhear this private conversation is obviously listening to a podcast or something.

"Do you think it's a virus?"

"Actually, I think I ate some bad meat."

A bell sounds in my brain and I scroll a little way down Petra's profile page. "Off to have lunch at JJ's Carvery. I love Sundays!" Okay, I've been to JJ's Carvery and found a suspiciously short and curly hair in my peas – food poisoning is seeming more likely than the pregnancy thing. That's disappointing. For a little while, I thought I had this big, juicy secret all to myself. Part of me is also very relieved that Petra won't have to have an abortion or a baby, but that's the old, soft me who actually gave a crap about other people.

"Ugh, I feel disgusting today," Petra whines.

"You don't look it," says Emily, in a reassuring tone.

"I didn't mean I feel like I look disgusting, I meant I feel all gross from throwing up."

"Oh. Well– "

"But now you're making me think I look disgusting as well as feeling disgusting."

"I said the exact opposite of that."

"I wish you hadn't said anything."

As Emily digs her own grave, it occurs to me that Petra in real life is different from Petra on social media. On social media, she's all inspirational quotes and relentless optimism, but now it seems like that's hiding a whole load of insecurities. This may not be a secret pregnancy, but it's still pretty interesting. I sit there with my headphones in, listening to every word.

little black book

The movie *Dead Tulips* is based on an old spy novel of the same name. It is now one of the three books on my Kindle. The other two are *Gone Girl* and *Looking for Alaska*. I don't read many book-length books because I have a crappy attention span. But I gobble up *Dead Tulips*, chapter by chapter, reading mostly at night when I can't sleep.

Paris, city of love. From what Lana had seen of it, she remained unconvinced; though perhaps she took a little more convincing than most women. The young bartender handed her a gimlet, or what passed for a gimlet in this place and time, and she aimed a smile at his hip pocket. She had good aim.

She swivelled around on her bar stool, sipped her watery drink and cast her eyes about for any sign of her contact. All she knew to look for was a dame with red hair and a blue dress. There was no guarantee she'd be pretty, or even young. Men who did unspeakable things were often looking for someone who could make them feel like a good person, as well as making them feel good. That was quite a trick, and often took many years to learn.

Time ticked away rapidly. The girl had better show up soon, or there would be hardly any time to talk before the ludicrous nine o'clock curfew. To ease her nerves, Lana watched the patrons of the bar. She didn't feel the need to be discreet about it, on account of how people-watching was practically a sport in this city; that was one thing the Nazis hadn't changed. Besides, the bar was dimly-lit and the air was so thick with smoke that she was probably half-hidden anyway.

Nobody in this bar was quite what they seemed to be. Of course, you could replace the word "bar" with "city", "country" or "world" and it would still be true, but wherever she was, Lana enjoyed figuring out what the people were hiding. The hollow-cheeked girl, laughing anxiously at some joke a shabby-suited man was telling; she was hunched over in an attempt to conceal the baby in her belly. The red-faced man, chattering raucously with two of his buddies; he was making a valiant attempt to drink all the liquor in Paris to stop his hands from trembling. The anaemic-looking blonde, waiting for someone at a corner table; Lana could tell from her shoulders that she knew some kind of martial art and could probably throw a fella halfway across the room if the mood took her.

Lana was about to let her attention wander somewhere else, when the blonde smiled brightly. Following the smile across the bar, Lana saw a tall, silver-haired man she had definitely seen somewhere before.

She studied his face, and heard the words "This is Dr and Mrs..." in her mind's ear. She had been introduced to the man and his plump, sombre wife at Eugène's party, or what passed for a party in this place and time. The doctor, whose name Lana couldn't recall, had talked about moving to the countryside. It wasn't the presence of the Nazis in Paris that bothered him so much as the unreasonable rationing of tobacco.

So the good doctor wasn't so respectable after all, meeting up with blondes in bars. This seemed like information that might be worth something in the future, so Lana reached into her purse and took out her little black book, her pen, and her tiny bottle of invisible ink. She wrote "Doctor (married friend of Eugène) spotted in bar with mystery blonde" in letters that glistened fleetingly on the page, then dried and disappeared.

"What are you writing?" asked the young bartender,

peering at Lana's book as he wiped a glass with a filthy rag.

"A love letter," Lana replied, in French of course. She made sure to keep her mouth demure, while letting her eyes suggest that she was writing something pretty wild.

The bartender's blush was clearly visible in the gloom. "A letter for a lucky man," he muttered.

"He is not lucky yet, but he will be lucky soon," said Lana, smiling sweetly.

Perhaps it was madness to be writing with invisible ink in public places, but Lana's little black book contained nothing to incriminate her. If anyone heated up the pages with a flame or a lightbulb, the brown scribblings that would appear were nothing but gossip. Trivial stuff. People's flirtations and drunken misdemeanors and affairs of the heart. The kind of thing only a feather-brained woman would be interested in. As for the invisible ink, that was only lemon juice – a sure sign of an amateur.

Lana stole a glance over her shoulder and saw a flash of copper across the bar. She stashed her little black book, pen, and ink back in her purse, then waved enthusiastically at the redhead as if they were childhood friends. The redhead only looked surprised for a second. She caught on quick and waved back, smiling warmly. It was best to be as familiar as possible. No matter what coded messages the girl relayed about her moderately high-ranking SS lover, Lana had to keep smiling like they were discussing wedding plans or shoes they could never afford. Due to her line of work, Lana did not have anyone she considered a friend. But *she knew how to pretend, and that was the important thing.*

ethan

chapter five

Petra Rawlins (size 8) thinks she is fat.

That was the first thing I typed up. In the Notepad app, on my phone. I'm not sure why I typed it up – probably most of the girls at school think they're fat, so it's hardly a jaw-dropping revelation. But it seemed funny and sad and worth documenting, somehow.

After that, I start typing up more things. Snippets of overheard conversation. Bits of gossipy nonsense that, upon further investigation, turn out to be true. This snatching and hoarding of information I'm not supposed to know gives me a buzz, like stealing pick 'n' mix when I was a kid.

At the back of the bus on the way home from school, I sift through the contents of my phone. I have a few interesting new photos, including a packet of tablets poking out of Serena Lawson's bag. If I zoom in, the packaging says "Sertraline" – I'll have to google that. Then there's a discreetly taken photo of Chris Langford's hand discreetly squeezing Amy Whitaker's thigh, under the table in Geography class, and another photo of Chris Langford snuggling up to Katie Fletcher in a corner of the library.

Lana Barrington has her little black book, written in invisible ink. I have my password protected phone. Both of us could do some damage with the information we have, if we wanted to.

The bus is getting close to my stop. I press the button and, as usual, the bus almost whizzes right past the stop. Bus drivers don't expect anyone to live here because you can't see any houses from the road – just fields and hedgerows. Sometimes, when the bus door opens at my stop, the smell of manure drifts in, and I have to get out quickly, face pink with embarrassment.

I cross the main road and start walking down the narrow, winding lane that leads home. It's a plain, grey day, but there are clumps of defiantly yellow daffodils blooming at the side of the road, and I'm not sorry to be outside.

Halfway down the lane, there is a five-barred gate that opens onto a field of short, sheep-nibbled grass. A familiar figure leans against the gate, staring down at his phone. As I approach, I tread lightly so as not to disturb him – I want the opportunity to watch him for a moment, without being watched in turn.

I swear Ethan gets taller every time I see him. He must be over six feet tall now, though he hasn't lost his puppy fat. His hair is still short and brown and nondescript. His skin has cleared up, but the acne he used to suffer from has left vindictive little scars all over his cheeks. He is wearing a *Game of Thrones* t-shirt under his jacket.

"Hi," I say, deliberately loud and sharp. He jumps a tiny bit, then looks up, confused for a moment.

"Oh my god, hi!" he exclaims, "I almost didn't recognise you, with the hair."

"What do you think?" I say, flicking it ostentatiously.

He cocks his head to the side and says nothing for a long moment, before saying decisively, "I like it." One thing that never changes about Ethan is his insistence on taking his time to answer questions. Sometimes this makes people think he's stupid, which is hilarious.

"So how have you been?" I ask.

"Not so bad. How about you?" I could answer the question honestly. I've been bored and lonely since my two best friends broke up with me for kissing this guy that one of them had a crush on for ages. So I took up a slightly unhealthy, morally questionable hobby to keep myself busy.

"Yeah, I'm good," I say, instead.

There's an awkward pause. I cover it up by hopping onto the gate and looking out into the field. I picture two kids running about, playing cops and robbers, dragons and princesses – all the games you play before puberty saps your energy and gives you a bunch of bullshit inhibitions.

Ethan turns around and rests folded arms on the gate. As if he's reading my mind, he says "Hey, do you remember that time when you completely covered me in stickyweed and that horse tried to eat me?"

"It wouldn't have eaten you, it would've just nibbled off all the stickyweed. And you got your own back anyway; you chased me around with horse crap on a stick."

He laughs sheepishly. "Were we horrible kids? I get the feeling we were horrible kids."

"Nah, we were just ... high-spirited."

"I hope you realise I've matured a lot since the horse poo chasing incident."

"I haven't."

"Really? You look more mature."

"I grew boobs."

"That's not what I meant! I meant... I don't know, the lipstick and stuff."

"So you didn't even notice them? Come on, I've been growing these things for six years. If you grew a beard I'd definitely compliment it."

I'm being mean, but it's so difficult to resist. He's adorably flustered now – mouth opening and closing like a fish. "Err, okay... it feels like things couldn't possibly get any more awkward than this so I might as well ask." – there's a sharp little hiss of breath being drawn in past his teeth – "Do you want to hang out sometime?"

"We're hanging out now."

"I mean hang out properly, at a restaurant or the cinema or something. This weekend, maybe."

I'm starting to feel weird. Unsteady, like the gate I'm standing on is swinging a little on its hinges. I look down and it's perfectly still. Only my insides are moving. "Do you mean a date?"

"Sure, why not?" There's a shrug in his voice but I can see tiny beads of sweat sparkling on his forehead, despite the nippy weather.

Why not? Oh God, I can't think of a reason. 'I don't want to' isn't a reason, it's a rejection. I can't tell him I have a boyfriend because he's got me on Facebook, where my relationship status is permanently set to single. Should I tell him I'm a lesbian? No, that would probably come back to bite me on the arse.

"Can I think about it?" I blurt out.

"Um, yeah. Of course. Just message me if you fancy it, yeah?"

"Yeah."

He walks off down the road and I keep clinging to the gate for a minute or two because I don't want to risk catching up with him.

I said I'd think about it, but as I walk home, I try to think about anything other than Ethan's offer. I think about the mysterious tablets in Serena Lawson's bag. I think about what I'm going to eat for dinner (there's some leftover cottage pie from yesterday, I'll microwave it). I think about movies – specifically, I think about *Dead Tulips* and Lana the spy.

Lana Barrington flirts with practically every male character in the movie, and in the book, but she sure as hell doesn't fall in love with any of them. Maybe she's not even attracted to any of them. She acts the part, biting her lip or letting the strap of her cocktail dress fall over her shoulder. She gets a lot of stuff bought for her: drinks, dinner, a pair of ruby earrings that go straight to the local pawn shop. Manipulative, maybe, but as Lana says, "A girl's gotta eat." And besides, if a guy wants you to kiss him or hook up with him or fall in love with him, he should just ask. He can't ask you out to dinner and expect it to turn into something other than dinner.

Ethan said he'd take me to a restaurant. There's a new Indian place in town that I've been dying to visit because the main menu features about a hundred authentic Indian curries, but the dessert menu has good old English apple crumble and sticky toffee pudding. Best of both worlds. My empty stomach growls and makes the decision for me. I WhatsApp Ethan and tell him yes.

a spy in the library

chapter six

Birchwood Comprehensive Secondary School is not a particularly good school or a particularly shit one. Because this is a pretty rural, sparsely-populated area, the kids at the school come from all over the place. Consequently, it's not a posh school or a chavvy school – some of the kids grew up with au pairs and violin lessons, others grew up in run-down council flats living next door to drug dealers. We always have a few Traveller kids who sometimes ride their horses to and from school, but they usually leave after Year 7 or 8. People get along, mostly. Not always.

The school buildings themselves, and the furniture in them, are mostly old and uninspiring. But the library was refurbished a couple of years ago, and there's now one particular corner of it that's a little piece of heaven. There are these ergonomic chairs that are easily comfy enough to sleep in, clustered around small tables. The radiators pump out heat in the winter and a huge window lets in sunshine and cool breezes in the summer. It's a highly sought-after spot.

When the librarians realised this, they put a sign up saying 'The seating area may ONLY be used for reading' because naturally, people were hanging out and chatting and playing games on their phones. The sign was later amended to 'The seating area may ONLY be used for reading actual BOOKS, made of paper' because people would insist they were reading e-books on their phones. Now, the accepted protocol is to pick a random book from the shelves, open it at a random page and then chat quietly or play on your phone discreetly. If a librarian comes over, you shut up and pretend to be completely engrossed in *A Beginner's Guide to Exotic Animal Husbandry* or whatever crap you've picked up without looking at the title.

I am currently lounging in one of the comfy seats, pretending to pretend to read *Wuthering Heights* while actually playing *Animal Crossing* on my phone. It's a double deceit, you see – Lana Barrington would be proud. I'm actually eavesdropping on a murmured conversation between Grace Bagshaw and Aoife McCall, who are sitting in the chairs opposite me, and writing occasional notes on my phone. Straining my ears to pick up everything Grace and Aoife are saying, I type, 'Bonnie Skidmore has a new boyfriend. Is it still called a boyfriend when the boy is a 26-year-old man?'

"They go to the same karate club", Grace mutters. "He's a brown belt, apparently."

"Oh, well that makes all the difference." Even in a near-whisper, Aoife's voice drips with sarcasm. "Christ, twenty-six. He might as well be thirty."

"Bonnie's not exactly an innocent little virgin, though, is she? She probably knows what she's doing."

"So does he take her to nice restaurants and get her into clubs and stuff like that?"

"I don't know. I only know that they went to the Ashford Spring Fair together and he won her a goldfish. It only lasted one day. The goldfish, I mean. It died."

"Wait, so... they went to the Ashford Fair... does this guy actually *know* he's Bonnie's new boyfriend? 'Cause remember what happened with Eric, back in Year 10."

I hide behind *Wuthering Heights* and soak up the gossip and speculation. I feel a sudden rush of nostalgia, remembering how me and Ethan used to hide behind *The Beano* and pretend to read, listening in on our parents' conversations, playing spies. One time we got a big, broadsheet newspaper and cut eye holes out of it, because we'd seen some cartoon character doing that.

I can't help but wonder why me and Ethan ever stopped hanging out. We were inseparable as kids, but we drifted apart when we were about eleven, and then we went to different secondary schools so we rarely saw each other after that. Why did we drift apart? Maybe we realised we were destined for different social groups. He's always worn the nerdy parts of him like badges of honour, whereas I don't fit in with proper geeks because I've never played Dungeons and Dragons and I have no strong feelings about the last season of *Game of Thrones*. Or maybe we just got annoyed with each other. Perhaps I got fed up with the way he can never make a quick decision, but has to chew it over from every angle. Maybe he got irritated with my impatience or my knack for getting myself (and him) into trouble.

I kind of wish I wasn't going on a date with him. I kind of wish we could just hang out instead.

date night

How are you supposed to feel, getting ready for a date? Excited? Nervous? I'm a little excited about prawn Balti and chocolate fudge cake but other than that, I don't feel anything. I can't be arsed with choosing the perfect outfit so I just pick my shortest dress, then put my face on and rush downstairs, already running late.

I'm meeting Ethan on the corner of Waxcap Lane, to spare him the trauma of having to talk to my parents. I've told them I'm going on a date, but I haven't told them who with because I don't want to risk gossip spreading around the village. They're actually being okay about it. Mum is just surprised that teenagers still go on dates – she thinks it's all sexting and Tinder these days. Dad wanted some reassurance that I know how to break a guy's nose (it's not rocket science – a sharp jab upwards with the heel of the hand will do it), just in case.

I'm out of the house before Mum has a chance to comment on my dress or my highly visible thighs. By the time I get to the corner of Waxcap Lane, Ethan is already standing there with his hands in his pockets, wearing a shirt with buttons. I've never seen him look so uncomfortable.

"You look…" I can practically hear his brain whizzing through various complimentary adjectives, and when he finally settles on "nice" I'm a little disappointed. Nice isn't the effect I was going for.

"You look good too," I offer, though honestly the shirt doesn't suit him as well as the *Game of Thrones* t-shirt did.

"Shall we get going then?" he says, sounding like he's in a hurry. Like he thinks we can outrun the awkwardness of this situation if we don't stay in one place for too long.

"Sure. And where exactly are we going?"

"We'll get the bus into town, and then I was thinking of a restaurant, if you're hungry."

"Sounds good. Which restaurant?"

"It's a surprise." He grins, and I arrange my face into an expression of contented excitement. I thought he'd let me choose, and I could pick the new Indian place. This is not going exactly to plan.

By the time we get to this surprise restaurant, things are not going to plan at all. Of all the stupid places to pick for a date, he's picked Mariana's. Mariana's is a cheap, shabby Brazilian place, where all the meat is grey. I mean, I've never been there before but that's what everyone says. I'd honestly rather go to McDonalds.

"It's got a great atmosphere," he insists, as we take our seats at a slightly wobbly table. I look around for a moment, soaking up the atmosphere that he speaks so highly of. There's lively music playing over speakers, but the place itself isn't exactly lively. In fact, it's practically empty. I look at the menu and understand why.

"God, they do some weird food here. Who eats chicken hearts?"

"Brazilians, I guess. It's no weirder than steak and kidney pie."

He's right, and I'm annoyed. I slump in my creaky wooden chair, running my eyes over the menu and thinking of chicken hearts. Despite my pet hens, I'll still happily eat chicken – just not those particular chickens because they have names and personalities and funny habits. But eating *hearts*, that's... A cold voice at the back of my brain tells me that hearts are just another muscle. Muscle = meat. Meat = muscle. I feel my own lump of meat beating a hollow, steady rhythm in my chest.

I order something that is apparently a beef and black bean stew. I've no idea what it is that Ethan orders, but at least it's not the chicken hearts. I'm in a rotten mood. I was planning on flirting with Ethan, but I don't feel like it now. It was supposed to be a kind of trade – he pays for a slap-up meal and in exchange, I stroke his forearm and run my fingertip over the rim of my glass and do all those things that men like, all while wearing the world's most uncomfortable bra. I guess the problem with this kind of 1940s-style arrangement is that the dude gets to make all the decisions.

"So, what made you choose this place?" I ask, half-heartedly. Silence. I look up from the menu and Ethan flashes a sudden, very green smile. He's taken the lime wedge out of his glass of water and is wearing it like a gum shield. Apparently I have all the sophistication of an eight-year-old, because this makes me laugh. When he keeps it in his mouth and tries to talk around it, I laugh even more.

The tension that's been clouding the air so far disappears. We talk about movies. We argue about who ought to be the next James Bond. He shows me some recent photos of Squiggle (his pet Labrador) on his phone and I consider reciprocating with a picture of the hens, but decide against it because I think the fried thingamajigs he's eating have chicken in them. He tries to convince me that I should give LARPing a go. I try to convince him to share his fried thingamajigs because the stew I ordered was a mistake.

When we've finished our meal, I make a completely bullshit gesture of reaching for the bill, which he grabs and pays without a fuss. We leave the restaurant and meander through the town, chatting about this, that, and the other. Somehow we end up holding hands – the kind of hand-holding where your fingers are intertwined and you're properly locked in. It doesn't feel any different to holding hands with Martine or Angie, but I'm acutely aware that it *looks* different. Anyone who sees us would probably assume we're a couple. I lift my chin and walk a little taller. I spend so much time feeling like a kid (albeit one with tits and cynicism), it's nice to feel grown-up now and again.

We catch the bus home and walk back to the corner of Waxcap Lane. It's a clear night with a skinny sliver of a crescent moon, and the stars look like … well, like stars. I suspect that going all poetic about starlight is something that only happens to you after you fall in love. Since that hasn't happened to me yet, stars are just sparkly dots and they don't evoke any particular feeling.

"I had a really good time tonight," says Ethan.

"Me too," I say, and I'm being mostly honest.

"Good. I wanted it to be special, you know, 'cause you're special." He's mumbling, embarrassed about being an absolute sweetie. It's cute, but the word "special" snags at something inside me.

"What do you mean, special?"

"I mean special in a good way, not special like … you know."

"Like when people say special and it kinda sounds like the r-word?"

He huffs, and says, "You know, you're ruining the moment here," but I'm determined to get to the bottom of this.

"Sorry, I just want to know what you mean by special. Do you mean, like, better than other people?"

"No, I mean…" he trails off, and I let him think because he doesn't like to think and talk at the same time. Usually he thinks first and speaks afterwards, but this seems to be one of those rare occasions when he spoke first.

"Okay, honestly I was trying to say a generic nice thing. But you're not interested in a generic nice thing because you're you. You're unique."

Well, shit. I think this is the moment where my knees are supposed to go weak. They don't, though.

"Everyone's unique."

"Yeah, everyone's unique but some people are *different*."

"You think I'm different? How am I different?"

"I don't know, it's difficult to put into words. But I mean that in a positive sense. It's good to be different. I'm different, and I wouldn't want to be … undifferent."

A sudden wave of affection washes over me and I hug him, almost fiercely. He hugs me back, wrapping his big, bulky form around me. When our grip on each other loosens and we pull away, I can see him leaning down to kiss me.

No. Not happening. No spit-coated lump of muscle wiggling about in my mouth, I am so not in the mood. I turn my face away and he kisses my cheek – lips slightly parted but mercifully dry. I aim a quick, bird-like peck at his cheek in return, then say "See you soon," and practically run the rest of the way home.

currency

chapter seven

Angie used to complain that I never had any decent gossip to share. Gossip, in her opinion, had to involve boys. Crushes, kisses, hands under tops or bras or skirts. I used to make stuff up sometimes, because she thought I was being secretive if I didn't have any dirt to dish. Then she and Martine would talk about me behind my back.

A date with a childhood friend is hardly the juiciest of gossip, but hey, I'm a teenage girl. Any scrap of information about my love life, sex drive or the state of my hymen is highly sought-after currency. Perhaps I can trade this information for some interesting titbits to add to the growing arsenal of notes and photos on my phone.

There's a weird sense of power that comes with having so much personal information at your disposal. As I walk into Drama class on Monday morning, I feel like I'm carrying a small explosive device in my pocket.

Drama class is held in one of the little "huts" on the edge of campus. I don't know why everyone calls them huts. They're not rustic or cosy or made of wood – they are functional grey boxes with springy floors and big mirrors for the Dance students. The class is mostly girls, and one of those girls is Bonnie Skidmore. She is with the twenty-six-year-old boyfriend who may or may not be aware that he is her boyfriend – I intend to find out.

Bonnie is currently perched on a stack of chairs at the side of the room, hunched over her phone in the way that every tall girl seems to hunch. We've probably got a while before Mr. Ackerly gets here (he's usually about five minutes late) so I sidle up to Bonnie, all set to make the most of the spare time.

Talking to people is easier when you're not worrying about what they think of you. I was never exactly shy – not shy like Martine, anyway – but I used to wonder what I looked like in other people's eyes, and it got distracting sometimes. Now, I'm done caring about that.

"Hiya," I say brightly to Bonnie.

"Hey Gwen."

"Nice weekend?"

"Yeah, really good thanks." She gives me what I think is intended to be a mysterious smile. It doesn't quite work because she has a very wide mouth, so she looks more like the Joker than the Mona Lisa.

"Did you get up to much?"

"Oh, this and that." There's a little pause, during which I remind myself not to seem too interested. "How about you?"

I shrug. "The usual. I did have a date though."

"Ooh, anyone I know?"

"Maybe…" I flash my cheekiest of smiles. Perhaps, if I think of something really embarrassing, I could make myself blush. All this acting practice ought to count as extra credit towards my Drama AS level.

"You're a dark horse. I always thought you weren't interested in *anyone*."

"Just a late bloomer I guess." This is what Angie used to say about me. It seems like a weird analogy for developing sexuality. As far as I'm aware, flowers don't ever want to screw anyone, before or after they bloom.

"Are you gonna tell me who it is?"

"Nope." I make a smug face, and Bonnie looks irritated. Good stuff, hopefully she's starting to feel competitive. Oh my gosh, I get it! Flowers get *pollinated* when they bloom. That's basically flower fucking. Or flowers being fucked by bees. Okay, back to the task in hand.

"Oh go on! At least tell me if he's in our year," Bonnie says.

"Ugh, the guys in our year are so immature."

"I know, right? Women mature quicker, it's a scientific fact. Men are basically still kids until they're at least twenty-five."

"So you've gone out with a twenty-five year old?" I do my best to look impressed, and that seals the deal. She tells me everything, starting with stolen glances across a crowded dojo, and ending with...

"...so people can think what they like, but older men are a hell of a lot more patient than guys our age. They take the time to ... warm you up, you know?"

"You mean he's, like, not pressuring you into sex and stuff?"

"Well yeah, older guys don't rush into it. They know what they're doing with..." she mouths a word, and it takes me a moment to figure out that the word is "foreplay".

Thankfully, Mr. Ackerly arrives at this point, ending a conversation that's got me equal parts intrigued and queasy. Like a gory horror movie. I'll type up as much as I can remember after Drama class.

The play we are currently studying is *Waiting for Godot*. It is unspeakably boring, and I've actually said as much to Mr. Ackerly because he's the kind of teacher you can be honest with. He's young – late twenties, I think – and has floppy hair and enthusiasm in buckets, which makes him seem even younger. Last week, when I had a moan about the interminable dullness of *Waiting for Godot*, he admitted that he felt the same way. Then we ended up chatting about classic movies and he insisted I had to watch some Hitchcock films. "You'll love them," he promised. "Hitchcock basically invented the psychological thriller."

At the end of class, he beckons me over to him and says he has a DVD for me to borrow. I follow him over to the props cupboard, while he chats animatedly about the film. "It's *The Birds*," he says. "Not Hitchcock's finest, but it's still a classic. Phobias are a recurring theme in his work, and *The Birds* is just so *visceral*."

"What does visceral mean?"

"It means ... something related to deep internal feelings. Or internal organs. See, that's what I like about you Gwen – if you don't understand something, you ask about it."

"That's 'cause I hate not understanding stuff. It's frustrating."

"Good. That curiosity, that urge to understand people – it's what makes a good actor."

"You think I'm a good actor?"

"One of the best in the class."

"There's only eleven people in the class, so am I, like, top three? Who's the best in the class?"

"Okay, there's curious, and then there's nosy."

He's rummaging about for the DVD, moving aside a fake fur coat, a headband with cat ears, Juliet's retractable plastic dagger, and muttering, "Where the hell did I put it?" I help him look, bending down to search a lower shelf. He reaches up to a higher shelf, and as he does so, he puts a steadying hand on my back. Quite low down. Right between the kidneys. I can feel the warmth of his hand through the thin material of my top, but it gives me a cold feeling in my guts. "There we are," he says triumphantly, pulling down a DVD and handing it to me.

The prop cupboard suddenly seems very small and cluttered, and I can't get quite enough air into my lungs. This is ridiculous. It was a hand on my back, that's all. Casual as anything. I don't think he even noticed.

"Thanks," I say, avoiding his eyes and looking down at the DVD case. A scared-looking blonde woman is running away from some birds.

"You're welcome," he says, and his voice is soft like snow. "You do have something you can watch it on, don't you?"

"Yeah, we have an old telly that plays DVDs. I'll probably watch it tonight, so I'll give it back to you later this week."

"No rush. It's yours for as long as you want it."

I don't want it. But it's in my hands now, so I don't have any say in the matter.

the friend zone

I watch *The Birds* on the old telly in Darren's room. It's deliciously creepy, even though I'm not usually spooked by birds at all. Except for swans. Those thick, snake-like necks and hissing beaks and the way everyone knows someone who knows someone who was attacked by one of them.

My phone buzzes, just as the birds are congregating eerily on a climbing frame in a playground. The message is from Ethan, and it reads "Hey sexy, how are you?" When he texted me yesterday it was "Hi gorgeous" and I replied with "Hi dude" trying to steer the tone of the conversation in a more platonic direction. Clearly, he hasn't got the message yet, so I type, "Hey bro, I'm good thanks. You?"

"Yeah, I'm good. Just thinking about you and wondering if you wanted to hang out again? Are you free tomorrow after school?"

I want to say yes, for two reasons. The first is that I am obviously free after school due to my sad, friendless state. The second is that I do actually want to hang out with him – he's clever and interesting and has this quietly adventurous spirit that I still remember from when we were kids. However, there are also two reasons for saying no: guilt, and the ick factor. He's obviously after a boyfriend-girlfriend thing and that's not going to happen, so if I say yes I'll be leading him on a wild goose chase. There's also a risk of him kissing me, and I don't seem to like kissing. Hopefully it'll get more enjoyable with practice, but I'm not practising with Ethan. He's not the sort of boy you practice on. Too damn sweet.

Okay, this is going to be awkward, but it looks like I'll have to clarify things. "I'd love to hang out dude, but this is just a casual thing, yeah? Not a date?"

There's a long pause, before he replies with "Shit,

you're friend-zoning me aren't you? This always happens. ☹"

Well, now I feel like crap on a croissant. As I'm struggling to string together some coherent, vaguely comforting words, he adds "Did I do something wrong?"

This one, at least, is easy to answer and I message back, "No, you did nothing wrong." I almost add 'It's not you, it's me' before remembering that people are usually bullshitting when they say that.

"How about we just take things slow? I promise I won't pressure you into anything you're not ready for, I just don't want you to put me in the friend zone."

The heavy lump of guilt in my stomach melts into bubbling anger. He doesn't get it. Nobody gets it. I don't even get it myself. My hands are sweaty as I type, "The friend zone is the only zone I have" then refuse to look at my phone until *The Birds* has finished.

I feel weird. It's like that feeling when you tell someone a big secret and you're all exposed and vulnerable for a minute, but then it starts to feel good. That being said, I'm still royally pissed off.

When the movie ends, I pick up my phone and read Ethan's messages. The first one is just a question mark. The second says, "What do you mean?" and the third says, "I don't understand, but if this is something you want to talk about, you can talk to me."

Bollocks I can. The light coming in through the

window is dimming, so I go outside to feed the hens. I scatter chicken feed on the grass, then crouch down to stroke June's soft feathers as she pecks at the ground, making contented clucking noises. June is my secret favourite, though I make sure not to give her any extra food or attention in case the others get jealous. Marjory is skittish, Helen is hyper, and Susie has a habit of pecking me viciously when I take her eggs, but June is calm and sweet-natured, and petting her is very soothing. In the twilight, surrounded by the familiar sounds of the hens, my tightly-wound mind relaxes enough to wander to odd places.

Are the hens unhappy in this tiny, all-female world of theirs? Are they unfulfilled without any cockerels to fall in love with? No, that's daft. Animals don't fall in love, only humans do. That's what makes us human. So I've heard. My thoughts are getting more and more slippery. Slip-sliding back in time.

I'm eleven. I'm at the Year 6 disco. I'm wearing the kind of make-up that eleven-year-olds wear – coloured goo with glitter in it. My hair is still its natural, rabbit-fur colour and I am a happy bunny because I fucking love to dance. I don't have to dance in any particular way yet. I don't have to look sexy or even cool – I can just throw myself around however the music dictates. Ethan is not enjoying the Year 6 disco as much as me, because he does not love to dance. He's propped up against the wall with a bunch of other boys.

The crowd of mostly girls on the dance floor gets slowly thinner as kids start to drift towards a corner of the school hall. A crowd is forming there, with kids sitting down on the floor. When I see Ethan detach himself from the wall to investigate, I decide to join him. "What's going on?" I ask him.

"I dunno," he says.

"We're playing spin the bottle," says Lily Seskis, and she grabs me by the wrist and pulls me down beside her. I grab Ethan by the wrist and pull him down beside me (this is easy, because he's still smaller than me).

I've never seen anyone my own age kiss before. Mostly it's shy little smooches and a lot of joke kisses (Jake Harewood, for example, blows a loud raspberry on Megan Bellamy's cheek) but there's a couple of proper snogs. Talia Sharpton and Adam Reeves kiss for eleven seconds.

"Did you know," says Ethan quietly, while we're waiting for Talia and Adam to finish smushing their faces together, "that not everybody in the world kisses. There's a lot of hunter-gatherer tribes who don't kiss, they think it's gross and weird."

I consider whether or not I think kissing is gross and weird. I guess I do, but I can't think that forever because I'm not in a hunter-gatherer tribe, I'm in England. The empty Dr Pepper bottle makes its way around the circle of kids, which has expanded to include all of us. When it gets to Ethan, he spins it so hard that it goes skidding right across the floor and he has to try again. He's biting his lip, like he always does when he's nervous.

I'm still focused on his chewed-up lower lip when he looks up at me. I look down at the bottle, and it's pointing inescapably in my direction. Everyone is murmuring and giggling. "Let's do a joke kiss," I whisper at Ethan.

"No, don't do a stupid kiss, do a proper kiss!" Lily Seskis squeals indignantly.

"Yeah, it has to be five seconds at least!" yells Adam Reeves.

I look at Ethan's round, difficult-to-read face, zooming in on his bitten lips. They make me think of tomatoes that are going soft and rotten. With his eyes still wide open, Ethan leans ever so slightly towards me. I spring up, turn around and run.

I run out of the darkened school hall and down the brightly lit corridor, then into the girl's toilets, where I lock myself in a cubicle. Breathing heavily, though I haven't run far, I put the toilet seat down and sit on it. I look down at my feet in their flat, silver shoes. When we went shopping for an outfit for the disco, I begged Mum for high heels, but now I decide I am never going to wear them. No matter how cool they look, shoes are no good unless you can run away in them.

That was the turning point. That was when me and Ethan started to drift apart. Maybe I humiliated him by running away. Maybe he actually wanted to kiss me and got upset that I didn't feel the same way. Maybe we both just realised that girls and boys being best friends is like one of those YouTube videos where a dog and a pig are best friends. It's cute, sure, but it's not natural.

other people's butterflies

chapter eight

Anyone who got a glimpse of my bedroom would assume that I'm a disorganized person. I'm not, though. It's all surface-level mess. Unmade bed, undies all over the floor, stuff like that. If you look closer, you'll see that everything has its place. Nothing ever gets lost in here.

I have the same attitude towards my phone. Everything has to be carefully organised and easy to find, especially since it's so full of other people's secrets these days. I am using up a Thursday evening sprawled across my bed, moving files around.

I used to have folders labelled A-G, H-S and T-Z, and the files within the folders would be labelled with people's names. I planned on having some information on every person in my year. A bit of overheard gossip, an incriminating photo, an interesting fact – anything really. I still want some information on everyone, I guess, but now I'm organising it differently.

I've created four folders, labelled "sad stuff", "sex stuff", "love stuff" and "miscellaneous", for the leftovers.

sad stuff

It seems like everyone in this school is sadder than they look. I mean, I guess there are a few people with resting bitch face who look sad all the time, but most people seem like they have everything sorted. There's the girls, with their Instagram pictures that look like scenes from a Lana Del Rey music video. Then there's the boys, who act like they're made of rubber. Like anything life throws at them will just bounce off.

It's not true though, and I know this must sound stupid but I never really realised it until I started prying into people's personal lives. There's plenty of stuff that never gets anywhere near social media. The pills in Serena Lawson's bag, for example (apparently Sertraline is used to treat depression and anxiety disorders, and my money's on anxiety because Serena's more twitchy than mopey) or the fact that Terry MacMillan's been seeing the school counsellor every week for the past couple of months (this is almost definitely connected to the rumours about his Mum running off to Spain with some bloke who isn't his stepdad or his dad, but I need to investigate further).

sex stuff

I once heard that the average man thinks about sex every six seconds. I never understood that. Like, does he think about sex for a second, then think about other stuff for five seconds, then think about sex for another second, then think about something else for another five seconds, etc.? Maybe it wasn't meant to be taken literally. Maybe it just meant that sex is never far away from a man's mind, and given how much everyone in my year talks about it, this seems pretty obvious.

When you get a group of boys together and they don't think any girls are listening (because, for example, you're hiding around the corner, pressed up nice and flat against the wall, but looking all casual like you're just waiting for someone) the stuff they say can be stomach-churning. Maybe that's just me being all squeamish and sexually stunted, but really, some of the crap they say is beyond the pale. The way they talk about girls they want to shag can be pretty violent – my personal least favourite is "I'd destroy that". Also, it seems like to be considered good in bed, a girl doesn't really have to do much, she just has to allow stuff to be done to her. Hayley Coldridge is apparently good in bed because she let Tony Parker jizz on her face.

The way girls talk about sex is different. It's messier. Less straightforward. I think most of the girls want it just as much as the boys, but they're more frightened. Frightened of pain, of getting into a situation they can't get out of, of what people will say about them; of something really bad happening to them, like on a TV crime drama or like the dead woman they found in Birchwood Forest a few years ago with a ten pound note stuffed in her fanny. It's no wonder, really, that girls want to make it *nicer*, with romance and mood lighting and feelings. No wonder Edie Richardson always lights those Yankee candles that smell of fresh linen every time she has sex with her boyfriend, and now she can't hang the washing up without getting turned on.

love stuff

Ooh, boy. "Love" might not be the best heading for this folder. "Attraction", maybe. I don't know what the crucial differences are between fancying someone, having a crush, falling for someone, and being in love – the whole shebang makes my head spin. But for simplicity's sake, I call it all love.

It's not so difficult to keep track of who's with who. It's understanding it that's the real challenge. Take Chelsea Pallotti, for example. She's been with James

Townsend since Year 10, and at some point she went through a pronoun change. She's not an I anymore, she's a We. "We love that movie, don't we?", "We're not busy this weekend." Stuff like that, all the time, as if they're the same person. They were named cutest couple in the Year 11 yearbook though, so maybe this is what a couple is supposed to be like.

As much as I like the giddy, powerful feeling of having all this dirt on everyone, I don't think I'm ever going to show it to anyone else. Seems kind of pointless, spreading it around to cause drama, and there's nothing I particularly want from anyone so I don't know how I'd use it to manipulate people. I'm just going to keep it, and it's going to help me understand. Maybe it'll help me learn how to feel the things I'm supposed to feel.

a proposal

chapter nine

Lana found Los Angeles to be a source of endless comfort, because it was always the same when she returned to it. She was rarely the same when she returned; on this occasion, for example, she had a new scar on her thigh and was poor for the third time in her life, having blown most of her money on bribing The Pig. Los Angeles, though, was just how she left it. The same cloudless sky. The same ocean breeze that tempered the heat of the day. The same social scene, where everyone acted as if they were drunk half the time and hungover the other half. There was a constant stream of bad decisions being made, and Lana made a point of documenting as many of them as possible in her little black book.

It was late on a Tuesday night and the bar was quiet. Just her and Ralph and a few committed booze hounds.

She'd been trying to cheer Ralph up, but he was as morose as ever on account of Jack leaving to join the army.

"He'll be back before you know it," Lana promised, doing her best to sound certain.

Ralph scoffed. "Don't count on it. He has no survival instinct. Likes the idea of being a hero; you know the type."

Lana did know the type, and had never understood them. She looked sideways at Ralph, whose eyebrows were knitted together in worry. There was something else. There was always something else.

"What is it?" she prompted.

"It's just that... even if he does come back, I know he's hoping that being in the army will... y'know, fix him."

"Oh."

"Yeah."

"Does that seem likely?"

For the first time that evening, Ralph almost smiled. "He'd take a hell of a lot of fixing."

Ralph took a crushed pack of smokes out of his pocket and put one between his lips. It was the way he held his cigarettes that had first made Lana realise he was a fairy. The same way her uncle Alric held them.

"You want one?"

"No thanks."

Lana didn't much like cigarettes, though they were a useful tool for flirting. Any cylindrical object that could be suggestively caressed would do, really. No matter how small. That always amused her.

Ralph blew smoke carefully away from her, then rested his chin in the palm of his hand. His eyes were glazed and a little bloodshot.

"Marry me?"

Lana was fairly certain she had misheard. "Excuse me?"

"Will you marry me?"

"You're drunk."

"I'm proposing."

"That's a terrible idea."

"It's a perfectly good idea, and you know it."

Lana cussed under her breath, then sipped her drink. She could scarcely believe she was considering this, but there were certain facts of life that could not be avoided. One of these was that the world was built for two. Another was that loneliness was dangerous and led to poor decisions.

Ralph was a good man. Lana had no moral compass of her own, so it would be helpful to borrow his. Also, he was never out of work and he made her laugh. Lana liked the idea of protecting him. A wife would give him a little more respectability. Keep him safe from rumours and gossip and those godawful vice cops who were so keen to bust in on any pair of queers having a good time, but if some fourteen-year-old girl got raped on her way home from school, they'd only shrug and say she was showing too much collarbone.

"Could I get an answer before Christmas?"

Lana forced her train of thought back on track and looked up at Ralph. He was still in the same casual pose, with *his chin in his hand. But his eyes were watchful and there was a slight nervousness around the corners of his mouth. Lana's heart sank. It was always a relief to know she still had one.*

"No. I'm sorry darling, but no. You and I, we're not built for marriage."

Ralph shrugged. Lana couldn't tell if he looked disappointed or relieved. "Well, I tried."

"I do appreciate it. Really, I do. But I think you should try to be happy instead."

"Hm. I'll drink to that."

They both drank deeply.

a party

c h a p t e r t e n

There are plenty of gossips in my year. There's Zoe Moses, who's permanently bored (seriously, put the girl on a rollercoaster or in a hostage situation and she'd probably still have that heavy-lidded, pouty look) and spreads any news she gets hold of in the hope that something vaguely interesting will happen. Then there's Katrina "KitKat" Banks, who is a grandmaster at faking niceness. She has a way of creating drama that always makes her seem like the good guy – the concerned friend, who says things like "The last thing I want is to stir shit up but I think you ought to know this because I hate that he's being so two-faced." There's also Elliott Chorley, who just gossips because he can. He has a lot of friends who are girls and a lot of friends who are boys, and he thinks it's funny to go back and forth like a double agent, spilling secrets.

The thing I don't like about gossips (and yeah, I know I'm not in any position to judge people, but whatever) is that they're incapable of keeping anything inside them. Their own opinions, other people's secrets, anything. They just spew it all out. Maybe I'm not a very well-adjusted person, but at least I'm not like that. I'm an expert at keeping things inside.

I get chatting to KitKat (AKA Katrina Banks) in the canteen queue because I need to find out more about Terry MacMillan's mum who ran off to Spain with her mystery bloke.

"Oh God, poor Terry!" KitKat exclaims dramatically, eyeing up the unpromising-looking sausage rolls. "I can't help worrying about him, it must have come as such a shock. What kind of a person does that? Runs off to a different country and leaves three kids behind. Terry's stepdad's completely useless too, so I've heard."

"Have you heard anything about the guy she ran off with? I mean, I know Terry's not running around telling everyone but if he needed a shoulder to cry on it'd probably be yours, right?"

"Well… you're not going to go spreading this around, are you?" KitKat ladles concern over her voice as the dinner lady ladles bolognese sauce on her spaghetti.

"No, of course not. You don't have to tell me anything, I just thought you might want to get things off your chest. You take on other people's problems a lot, maybe too much." Mwahaha, I am the queen of Bullshitland.

"Yeah, I know. Let's wait until we're sitting down so *people* don't overhear." This is clearly directed at the dinner lady, who rolls her eyes in irritation.

When we're seated at a wobbly table, right in the middle of the canteen, KitKat smiles her feline smile and eagerly picks up the scandalous subject. "God, you're not going to believe this. The man she hooked up with, right – she never even met him before she ran off to Spain!"

"What? How– "

"They only met online."

"So he could be, like, a fourteen-year-old boy or a con artist or something."

"No, he's her age. And he hasn't conned her out of any money – not yet, anyway."

"But that's insane! She's messing up her whole life for a guy she never met."

KitKat shrugs, twirling spaghetti round her fork. "Well, that's love – it makes people do crazy things."

"Then why do people want it so much?"

KitKat giggles, but then she sees the humourless expression on my face and looks confused. "You're joking, right? Love is… it's the point of it all. What else is there?"

I want to answer her, even though this is clearly a rhetorical question. I want to tell her there is a ton of other stuff, there has to be. But there's a cold lump of panic forming in my throat and I can't get any words around it.

"So are you going to Jodi's birthday party?" KitKat asks.

"Huh?"

"You know, Jodi's seventeenth. She's throwing a house party. Oh shit, were you not invited?"

"No."

"Please don't feel bad, it's not like she invited everyone."

"It's fine, I wasn't expecting– "

"You know, I bet if I had a word with Jodi I could convince her to invite you."

"You don't have to, I don't really– "

"Oh, it's no problem. Happy to help." KitKat smiles, sweet as syrup, and looks like she means it.

My mum once told me, after a few glasses of wine, that I should never turn down an invitation to a party. Then she back-pedalled and said I should turn the invitation down if the party was at a crack house, or if the invitation was given by a creepy old man. "You have to say *yes* to life, Gwen," she said, all glassy-eyed and unfamiliar. "You know, I met Dad at a party. I almost didn't go."

I'm at Jodi Tustin's house party. I'm not intending to hook up with the future father of my kids, and I'm not saying *yes* to life. I'm here to snoop and spy and take sly photos and get all the dirt on everyone. Sorry, Mum.

There are a lot of people here. So many, in fact, that

there's nowhere at all to sit down in what Jodi calls the "lounge". Not even the arm of a sofa to perch on or a patch of floor to drop a cushion on and park your arse. I'm standing against the wall with a glass of fizzy, fruity, weakly alcoholic stuff, watching life's rich tapestry unfold.

At the moment, all the characters in life's rich tapestry seem to be trying to hump each other. Hands on forearms, biceps, lower backs. People making out in corners or draped over each other on the crowded sofa. There's music on, but nobody's dancing properly. A few girls are wiggling about a bit. I take a swig of my fruity drink. When I was younger, I always wanted to drink the kind of cocktails that women on telly drank. The kind that were pink or purple or blue and had orange slices on the rim of the glass and looked as though they tasted of Haribo. Now, I wish I could handle neat spirits. If I could do shots without feeling like I've been shot in the throat, I could get drunk nice and quickly.

I'm bored. There is nothing new happening in this room (the couples making out are already couples) and I can't hear any individual conversations; it's all just a tangle of voices. I push away from the wall and weave through the room, between the bodies. I pause for a moment as I pass the sofa, leaning casually on the back of it to see what Zoe Moses is looking at on her phone. She's messaging Elliott Chorley, saying "Come and find me sweetie I'm so bored!" Good to know I'm not the only one struggling to enjoy this.

I down the rest of my drink and leave the empty glass on the mantelpiece as I scuttle, crab-like, out of the room. I could leave the party, but it would feel like a waste of an evening. Instead, I head up the stairs. I've never been inside Jodi Tustin's house before, so I might as well explore.

The hubbub of noise from downstairs gradually fades. The landing is wide, and on one side of it there is a bookcase full of fat historical romance novels. If Martine had been invited to this party she would be up here by now, having a sneaky read. On the other side of the landing are doors, one of which is slightly ajar. I peer through the gap and realise it is Jodi's bedroom. Quick and quiet, I slip inside.

It might just be the fruity drink, but I'm starting to buzz. Being inside someone's bedroom is kind of like stepping inside their brain. Jodi's bedroom is neat, with sugar-pink walls and black-and-white posters of old screen starlets like Audrey Hepburn and Marilyn Monroe. There's no clutter anywhere – her things must all be tidied away inside the big white wardrobe and matching chest of drawers. There's no dirt or dust or half-drunk cups of tea or plates with crumbs on it. But as I look around the room, it dawns on me that there are still things in here that nobody is supposed to see.

The room's got layers, like an onion. There are the things you're supposed to see – stuff you can see from the doorway, like the posters and the duvet cover with little

Eiffel Towers on it. Then there are the things that need to be looked for, like the picture of Chris Hemsworth sellotaped to the side of her bedside table. There's a whole, complete person in this room, but a lot of it is probably hidden away inside drawers. And I can't go opening Jodi's drawers, can I? That's crossing a line.

Her wardrobe, then. That's probably just clothes, anyway. I open it up, and get startled by a tatty, one-eyed teddy bear on the floor of the wardrobe. He stares at me with his glassy eye. I get my phone out and take a picture and wonder why people are always hiding the sweetest parts of themselves.

I don't have the luxury of wondering for long, because there are footsteps on the stairs. I freeze. Probably just someone going to the bathroom, but... nope, they are coming this way. And there are two pairs of footsteps and the wardrobe is too full to hide in and I can't think of an excuse for being here. In a mad panic, I throw myself onto the bed and curl up in a foetal position. The sound of giggling leaks around the edges of the door.

I force myself to breathe slowly and deeply as the door opens. "Oh shit," says a male voice.

"Cheeky cow, sleeping on my bed," says the giggler – it's Jodi. I figure I'm about to be shaken awake, but nothing happens. There's a moment's silence, then the sound of kissing. A wet, sucking sound, like getting your shoe stuck in mud and pulling it out.

"Are you gonna wake her up and get rid of her?" says

the guy. I recognise the voice now – it's Big Jimmy.

"Nah, she looks all cute and peaceful." I don't feel remotely peaceful – my heart is going a mile a minute. There is a soft thud, then some more squishy noises. I think Jodi and Jimmy are making out against the wall. This is definitely some valuable gossip for my collection, but I still wish it wasn't happening. There is a moment of suspenseful silence, then, "Didn't you go out with her once?"

"No!" says Jimmy, a little too emphatically for my liking. "I mean, we kissed once but that was it."

"Was she a better kisser than me?" Jodi's voice has that half-joking thing going on.

"Honestly? She might just be the worst kisser in the world."

Jodi laughs explosively, but the laughter gets muffled quickly, like she's buried her face in Big Jimmy's chest. I shouldn't care. I shouldn't even be surprised – it wasn't exactly great for me either. The idea of being a bad kisser doesn't bother me, but I don't like the idea of being a bad actor. I should've been able to fake it. To convince him that I'm normal.

"What was so bad about it?" asks Jodi.

"She was just really... stiff. Like, her whole body went rigid."

Jodi snickers again, and I suspect Jimmy is doing an impression of me. "Do you think she's frigid or something?"

"Maybe. She was probably just nervous."

Nervous. For some reason, this pisses me off more than anything. Does he think I'm *afraid* of him? I'm not afraid of his stupid tongue. I'm not afraid of being kissed or touched or fucked or fallen in love with, I just don't *want* any of it. I'm itching with frustration and seconds away from popping up and saying all this out loud, when Jodi says, "Come on, let's go back downstairs," and Jimmy makes a disappointed noise. Then I hear the bedroom door open and close.

I lie there on the bed for a little while longer, to make sure my fake nap is convincing. Jodi's hastily muffled laughter rings in my ears like an echo, and it's still there when I get up. Maybe that's why I open the top drawer of her bedside table and peer inside. Socks and tights. The second drawer is full of undies – mostly black and lacy and uncomfortable-looking. The third drawer is a jumble of things that no-one else is supposed to see. Tampons, condoms, a book called *The Dominant* with a suspiciously bland picture of piano keys on the front cover. I take a photo of the contents of the drawer, close it, then head downstairs.

I manage to make it out the door without having to talk to anyone. After a quick bus ride and a long walk from the bus stop, I'm back home and in a foul mood. It's not late, but I stomp straight upstairs to my room anyway. Dad shouts "How was the party?" from the living room and I shout back "Okay!"

My room is even more of a mess than usual. Clothes everywhere. Half-drunk mugs of cold coffee on every surface. Bright, clashing, cartoon colours that I picked out back when I knew who I was. I start tidying it – hanging up clothes, organising drawers, straightening things out. Maybe if my room is less of a mess, my head will be less of a mess.

The bottom drawer of my chest of drawers always sticks, so I take out everything inside it – old make-up, Christmas wrapping paper, curling iron, Harley Quinn comics, glass jar that used to be full of sweets – and fish around, looking for the problem. There's a bit of paper or card or something stuck at the back. I give it a sharp tug and it comes loose.

It's a birthday card. A really, really old one that says "8 Today!" and has a picture of a little girl wearing roller blades. I open it up, and the writing inside is big and wobbly. It reads, "Happy birthday your my best frend love from Ethan XXX" My face crumples like a scrunched up piece of paper and I start to cry.

angie and martine

I am fifteen going on sixteen (Isn't that a song from *The Sound of Music*?) and so is Martine, and Angie has just turned sixteen. On her sixteenth birthday, she gained a

Pandora charm bracelet that she'll probably never wear because it's too girly, and lost her virginity. She didn't have much innocence left anyway, and with all the gymnastics she used to do, her virginity was probably even more of an abstract concept rather than a physical thing. Still, it's a big step.

The three of us are sleeping over at Angie's house, and are squashed onto her bed (this is not where the sex happened, luckily – that happened round her boyfriend's house) in our PJs, half-watching *Riverdale* on Angie's laptop and discussing Angie's newly-acquired sex life. Martine is fascinated. I kind of am too, to be honest.

"Did it hurt?" asks Martine.

"Yeah, it hurt like hell," says Angie, with relish. "I don't think it hurts that badly for everyone, though. We probably should've taken it more slowly, but I got impatient. Also, Ray's a big boy. I got on top the second time and it hurt less."

"How did it happen?" I ask, genuinely intrigued.

"Err, he put his dick in my vagina."

"No, I mean... how do you go from hanging out with someone to having their bits inside your bits? I just... I don't understand how it happens." Angie and Martine are both looking at me funny now, like I've said something stupid. Maybe I have.

"It just happens naturally," says Angie in a reassuring voice. "When you're with the right guy, anyway."

"What's the best thing about it?" asks Martine.

"I'm not sure. It's nice feeling that close to someone. And knowing that somebody wants you and thinks your naked body is hot, that's pretty awesome."

Huh. I kind of thought she'd say orgasms. Orgasms, as I have recently discovered, are the bees' knees. And not difficult to get on your own. It's starting to confuse me, why girls go to all the trouble of getting a boyfriend for sexual pleasure. I know boyfriends have other functions of course, but if you have friends for love and support, and your own fingers or maybe an electric toothbrush for orgasms, what exactly are you missing? There must be something. Otherwise the human race would die out.

I've been thinking about Martine and Angie a lot this week. I have no idea what's going on with them these days, and it sucks. I used to know basically everything, from what Martine ate for breakfast to the fact that Angie's dad has been having an affair for several years and her mum is aware of it but lets it slide for some reason. Now, I see them around school and have no fucking clue what is going on in their lives. Martine might have stopped worshipping those clean eating influencers and started scoffing bacon sarnies for breakfast. Angie's mum might have finally snapped and forced her dad to give up his mysterious mistress.

The two of them are more difficult to snoop on than anyone else. Since we have been avoiding each other, I can't exactly hang around nearby and eavesdrop on their conversations – they'd get suspicious. And I can't do social media stalking because they both blocked me when we broke up.

The opportunity arises during a sticky June lunchtime. The sky is pearly grey and there is something charged about the air, like there's going to be a thunderstorm. This is the kind of weather where boys get into fights. There was already a handbags-at-dawn scuffle between two tiny Year 7s this morning.

I eat lunch in the canteen. Slowly and unenthusiastically, because I've got no appetite for anything but ice cream in this kind of weather. The big canteen windows are open to let the breeze in, but there's no breeze. When I've given up on my lunch, I head outside and wander around in search of fresh air. It is nowhere to be found.

Behind the drama huts, right on the edge of the school grounds, there is "The Court". Sounds very grand, but it's just a multipurpose sports court, used for netball, basketball, tennis, badminton, and occasional, illicit games of British Bulldog. There's a high chain-link fence all the way around it, which makes it look like it'd be good for cage fighting. Which is what British Bulldog usually descends into.

At the moment, there's a basketball game going on.

It's all boys and all sixth-formers, and none of them are any good. Basketball isn't played with any regularity in PE lessons at Birchwood. It's mostly football and rugby for the boys, netball and hockey for the girls. The game is messy and chaotic, but that hasn't stopped spectators lining up along the chain-link fence and cheering and jeering as the mood strikes them.

There are benches on three sides of the court – a little way back but close enough to see what's going on. I take a seat on one of them, and notice Angie on the opposite bench, on the other side of the court. She's sitting by herself. It's unusual to see her without Martine at lunchtime – she must be off sick. Angie is leaning forward, hands on the edge of the bench, transfixed by the basketball game. She's always been sporty – maybe she understands what the hell is going on and who is winning. Then again, maybe she doesn't care and she's just enjoying watching the boys run and jump and sweat.

Suddenly, she springs up and heads over to the court, leaving her bag tucked under the bench. She yells something at one of the boys, who messes up a pass and hits another one in the face with the ball. Then there's a lot of shouting and the guy who got hit in the face leaves the court, cupping a hand over his nose. I can't hear anything that's being said, but it seems like Angie is offering to replace him. Eventually, her offer is accepted and she opens the big, clanking gate and enters the court. I'm already up and heading towards the bench where Angie has stashed her bag. Risky, with so many people around, but they're all watching the basketball game, and when else am I going to get a chance like this?

As I'm circling the court, I keep a cautious eye on Angie. She doesn't see me – her attention is laser-focussed on the ball. She's giving it her all, and though we don't even like each other anymore, I get this little twinge of pride watching her kick arse on the court.

I reach the bench with Angie's bag underneath and sit down. My heart is hammering. No-one is looking at me – everyone lined up along the chain link fences is watching the game. I push the bag out from under the bench with my foot, then reach down and frisk it, patting the outside pockets and feeling for something phone-shaped.

Stop acting shifty, I tell myself. Act like you own the bag, the phone, act like you own the whole sodding world. I unzip a side pocket of Angie's bag and pull out her phone, then force myself into a relaxed position, leaning back a little on the bench.

The background of Angie's phone is a picture of her and a boy I don't recognise. He's got sandy-coloured hair and he's kissing Angie's cheek. Angie has a big, triumphant smile on her face. The word "conquest" floats through my brain, and for the first time in forever I get the feeling that girls and boys are basically the same. We just brag about slightly different things in slightly different ways.

Okay, so Angie has a new boyfriend. What about Martine? I check Angie's WhatsApp messages and quickly find Martine's name. Their last conversation goes like this:

Do you think Mr. Ackerly is fit?
Angie? *poke poke*

Who?
I don't know who you're on about Sweets.

He was Gwen's drama teacher. He still is, I suppose.

You don't take drama
how do you know him?

The art club is making props for A Midsummer
Night's Dream. I took him a paper mache donkey's head.
We got chatting after that
Angie? You still there?

Yep. So what exactly do teachers chat about?

We had a really long conversation about books. :)
He doesn't seem much like a teacher.
He doesn't talk down to you.

Snore! Do you like him?

Of course, he's gorgeous!

He recommended a whole bunch of books.

I'm going to read every single one. :)

If you want to get his attention

just start wearing low-cup tops.

Show off the puppies!

You're incorrigible.

Don't know what that means.

But probably, yeah. :P

I think of Mr. Ackerly's hand on the small of my back in the props cupboard. I tell myself, for maybe the seventh time, that it was nothing. People touch people, it's no big deal. Richard Green stroking my thigh under the table in a Year 10 Religious Education class. That plumber who touched my waist as he squeezed past me to get to the sink in our tiny kitchen. What separates that stuff from Dad rubbing my back when I'm stressed out, or Martine resting her head on my boobs when she got sleepy watching a movie? There's no difference, except for the way it feels.

The sky darkens, and I hear thunder rumbling softly in the distance.

shit hits the fan

chapter eleven

My phone is missing. I'm on the bus, on the way home from school, going through every crevice and hidden pocket of my bag for the fifth time and finding nothing but dust, fluff, half a paracetamol and a cherry-flavoured lip balm I'd forgotten about. Over the last month or so, I've really gone to town with collecting information – snooping through people's phones and generally being a total creep – and the results have been worth the effort. I think about all those clearly labelled folders full of information. All those photos, all those notes, all those carefully concealed bits of other people's lives. Panic wells up in me.

I talk to myself in my mum's voice. Not out loud, obviously, because that would freak out the other people on the bus. But inside my head, I say, 'Take a deep breath. Now, this isn't the end of the world. Your phone is password protected, so there's no need to panic. When do you last remember seeing it?' I comb through the details of my day, but everything is tangled and confusing. Okay, relax. Chances are, someone has already found it by now and handed it in to the lost property office. Everything will be fine.

Everything is not fine.

"Are you sure?"

"Yep, we've definitely not had any phones handed in recently. We've collected quite a few over the years, though. There's a Nokia 3310 that's been in the box for… well, it was already there when I started working here, and that was ten years ago. We just keep hold of it for the nostalgia, you know."

"That's not my phone," I snap, feeling bad because this isn't Mrs. Kayani's fault, but anxiety is making me impatient. "My phone's pretty distinctive, it's got a cover with a picture of Detective Gecko on it."

"Who?"

"From the web comic. He's a lizard. Who solves crimes."

Mrs. Kayani looks baffled. "I'll keep an eye out for it."

I'm about to ask her to call me if it turns up, but stop myself just in time.

I spend the rest of the morning trying not to think about it and failing. What if it's lost forever? I was actually starting to understand people better, thanks to the information on that phone. I was solving all these little everyday mysteries, like why Harry Thoreau and Pete Jackson are BFFs most of the time but have nonsensical arguments every Computer Science lesson. It's half to do with their conflicting opinions on the best ways of debugging code, and half to do with the fact that they both have the hots for Kerry Bennet, who sits right between them and seems blissfully unaware of their competing attempts to get her attention. Wait… The computer room. I was there yesterday; maybe my phone fell out of my pocket. Maybe it's just sitting under a bench in a tangle of dusty cables, waiting for me.

As soon as the bell rings for lunch, I make a dash for the computer room. It's mostly empty, but that won't last long. I was sat by the window yesterday. Which row? Somewhere in the middle. I check under benches, getting right underneath them where the stuffy air of the room is at its hottest and dustiest. A speccy Year 7 boy reading a Batman comic online gives me a look, and I ask him if he's seen a phone lying around – more as an explanation for my weird behavior than a genuine attempt to get some help.

Eventually, I have to admit defeat. My phone isn't here, my throat is scratchy from all the dust I've inhaled, and I am suffering social media withdrawal symptoms. At least I'm in the right place to deal with the latter problem.

I grab a seat at the nearest computer and log into Facebook. Huh. A friend request. Been a while since I had one of those. I click on it, and quickly get this uncomfortable, queasy feeling that something is not right.

There's no photo, and the name of this person is "MimiKnowsStuff". Who the hell is Mimi and what exactly does she know? I accept the friend request and examine her profile. There's just one post, and it reads:

"Hey kids. Here's a fun fact to brighten up your morning. Edie Richardson gets turned on by the smell of fresh laundry. You can blame this sexual quirk on Yankee Candle, for making "Fresh Linen" scented candles that Edie uses to set the mood during sexytimes with her boyfriend. Don't be too embarrassed Edie, I have plenty of fun facts about other people too. Stay tuned. XXX"

That queasy feeling has turned into full-blown nausea because that "fun fact" came from my phone. Mimi, whoever the fuck she is, has my phone. She's broken through the password protection and dived right into all my precious information. To stop myself from wanting to throw up, I try to convince myself that Mimi found this out some other way. Maybe it's just a coincidence that my phone has gone missing at the same time this Mimi chick has decided to make mischief. Maybe Edie's turn-ons are actually common knowledge.

Another post pops up. It reads:

"Fun fact #2. Ralph Davies has a crush on Elsa from

Frozen. Ralph, she's a Disney character, she's not real. You need to let it go. #sorrynotsorry"

Okay, it's not a coincidence. Mimi definitely has my phone, and it's only a matter of time before she posts a "fun fact" about how Gwen Foster has been spying on everyone like a crazy, indiscriminate stalker. Shit, shit, shit.

ambush

Lana shivered in the sharp night air and pulled her coat around her more tightly. She longed to be wearing something warmer than the low-cut green dress underneath her coat, but she had to look as though she were anticipating an illicit rendezvous; why else would a woman be out here at night? She shifted her weight on the uncomfortable bench and glanced around, looking for any sign of movement. This was a wooded part of the park, with nothing but trees and a narrow path running through them. Outside the pool of weak artificial light created by the street lamp beside the bench, the darkness was thick as tar.

Berlin still had its charms, but Lana did not consider this park to be one of them. She was ill at ease in the countryside or any part of a city that resembled the countryside. People and buildings and roads; those were things she understood. The rhythms of plants and animals were strange and unpredictable, and a large area of land with no people in it was somehow overwhelming.

A loud flapping noise, like someone shaking rain from a hat, came from one of the trees behind her and a shiver worked its way from the roots of Lana's hair right down to her toenails. It was only a bird, of course, and Lana scolded herself for being so faint-hearted. She was wondering whether a cigarette would soothe her nerves when the corner of her right eye caught something moving, further down the path.

A figure came into view. As it passed beneath a street lamp, Lana saw exactly what she expected to see: a man in a camel-coloured coat. Relieved, she watched him stray from the path a little, pull a large envelope out of his coat, and deposit it at the base of a tree trunk. Then he straightened up, turned around, and disappeared into the gloom.

Lana slid from the bench and walked briskly down the path. She did not know the man's name or anything else about him, but she knew which tree he had placed the envelope under. The one with the twisted roots, that somehow looked like a doorway to a strange church.

As expected, the envelope was nestled in those gnarled old roots like an egg in a nest. She bent to retrieve it, but as she tucked it carefully inside her coat, she heard a noise that made her blood run cold. A small clicking sound, like someone stepping on a twig. A twig made of metal.

With her hand still inside her coat, she reached for her

gun. The moment her fingers were securely wrapped around the grip, she whipped around. The gun pointed at empty space. Either side of that empty space were two men – one of them wearing a camel-coloured coat and the other wearing an instantly recognisable uniform – pointing guns at her.

Two against one. Difficult, but not impossible. Others had lived to tell the tale. Lana trusted her neat little gun, from its endearingly stubby barrel to the homemade dum-dum bullets in the cylinder. She held it steady, eyes flicking from one shadowed face to the other. The men were both tall and heavy-set, but their faces were youthful. Inexperienced. She had a chance.

And then, all of a sudden, she didn't. A scuffling noise behind her was followed quickly by a blow to the back of the head, and all the stars in the sky seemed to rain down on Lana's eyelids as she fell to the ground.

the mysterious mimi

chapter twelve

It has been two weeks now, and without fail, Mimi has posted two or three times a day. More and more people are adding her on Facebook. Even those who don't have Facebook are signing up just so they can see what she posts. She's a sensation, and we all watch her profile like a hawk. No, not like a hawk. Like mice watching a hawk.

It's weird – I always thought of the contents of my phone as being some kind of explosive. But this isn't an explosion, this is more like a slow crumbling. I've heard girls crying in the toilets. People getting into arguments. Everyone staring daggers at everyone else.

Oddly, Mimi seems to be holding back. The stuff she posts is embarrassing, but I've got way worse on my phone. Stuff that could send people into hiding or end lifelong friendships or even (in the case of Liam

Bradbury's experiments with hydroponic weed) get them into trouble with the police. I'm sure she's ruined plenty of people's day, but she doesn't seem to want to mess up anyone's life. Maybe she actually has some kind of moral boundaries. Or maybe she's just saving the big stuff for later.

Who the hell is she? This is the first thing I think of when I wake up and the last thing I think of before I fall asleep. There are no obvious clues. Since there's no-one called Mimi in the entire school, I wondered if it was short for something. According to Wikipedia, it can be short for Miriam, Maria, Mary, Emilia and sometimes Emily. There's an Emily in my tutor group – Emily Holbrook. She's best mates with Petra Rawlins, who I thought was pregnant once upon a time. It's hard to imagine Emily as Mimi. She's sweet and scatterbrained and Mimi is clearly neither of those things. Also, she has a habit of leaving her bag on classroom tables without zipping it up, which isn't something I'd do if I was in possession of someone else's phone and was using it for nefarious purposes.

It's hard to concentrate in lessons these days. Whichever class I'm in, I find myself looking at people's faces, trying to find the best possible match for Mimi the shit-stirring phone thief. It must be someone tech-savvy, since they would've had to get around the password protection on my phone. Maybe someone in my Computer Science class. Interestingly, this class is mostly boys, which makes me wonder if the name Mimi was chosen by a boy to avoid suspicion.

I drive myself crazy with frustration trying to figure out who Mimi is, but it's better than the alternative. The alternative is guilt. Constant, gut-churning guilt, because this whole situation is at least 50 percent my fault.

"OK kids, here's a little quiz for you. See if you can figure out who owns both this very adorable teddy and this very naughty book."

The post includes the photos I took of Jodi Tustin's one-eyed teddy bear, and that book called *The Dominant* in her bedside table drawer. I feel like a heap of shit. I'd be embarrassed if people found out I still read Jacqueline Wilson books, and now people are going to find out about Jodi's kinky reading material, thanks to me. I try to convince myself that it's no big deal. That people read books like that on the bus sometimes. But clearly Jodi doesn't read it on the bus, or she wouldn't have hidden it away in a drawer.

Someone takes a seat at the computer next to me and says, in a voice breathless with concern, "God, isn't it awful?" I turn to see KitKat (AKA Katrina Banks, AKA Toxic Shit-Stirrer) sitting there, with a frown that doesn't reach her eyes.

"Yes," I say, with a little sliver of ice in my voice.

Whoever this Mimi chick is, she's no worse than KitKat. KitKat spreads everyone's personal information around and has the audacity to act like she's the nicest person in the world. "Do you have any idea who Mimi is? I mean, people confide in you a lot, so I thought maybe you'd heard something."

"If I found out who it is, I'd tell you in a heartbeat. Actually, I wouldn't just tell you, I'd tell everyone. It's bloody horrible what she's doing; she deserves whatever's coming to her."

"You say *she*, but do you think it could be a guy, maybe? Apparently some people can look at a piece of writing and tell whether it was written by a guy or a girl, but I can't do that. Do you know anyone who can?" I'm grateful to have someone to discuss this with – even KitKat.

"Hm? No," she says, staring at my computer screen. "Who do you think they belong to?"

"What, the teddy and the book?"

"Yeah."

"Does it matter? Everybody owns a couple of old teddies and a cheesy romance novel or two. I don't see what the big deal is."

KitKat laughs. "I love how innocent you are. That's not a romance novel, it's, like, S&M. Whips and chains and stuff."

"So?" I'm starting to blush, and I can't tell if it's from embarrassment or irritation.

"So, don't you think that stuff's disgusting?"

I want to tell her that yes, I think sex with handcuffs and spanking is kind of gross, but I also think sex with classical music playing in the background and rose petals on the bed is kind of gross. I want to tell her that it's all a big icky mystery to me and I don't understand why people get so excited and uptight and judgemental and obsessed about something that, by all accounts, doesn't even last that long. But obviously I can't say stuff like that to one of the biggest gossips in the school, so instead I say, "It's not my cup of tea, but I'm not gonna judge. Different people get turned on by different things."

KitKat sniffs sulkily, scrunching up her little button nose. "I just don't think it's *healthy*." She turns away, and I refocus on Mimi's post. A horrible realisation rolls down my spine like a drop of cold sweat. Jodi is going to see this post, and she's going to know that someone took pictures of stuff in her room. She saw me at the party, fake-sleeping on her bed. Granted, there were plenty of other people there and I'm sure she's had a bunch of other people in her room at one time or another, but what if she suspects me? What if she thinks I'm Mimi?

I have a sudden urge to go home early and just stay there forever. Clearly I shouldn't be around people because I am incapable of being a proper, normal person. First, though, I have to sort this mess out.

cyberbully

"Well kids, this has been fun. Now that I've got everyone's attention, here's a fact that is slightly less fun. Mr. Ackerly (he teaches Drama) is not safe. Do not allow yourself to be alone with him and warn your friends and siblings not to be alone with him. He is a creep and a predator. Have a nice day. XXX"

It spreads through the lower sixth in wide-eyed whispers, and within a week it has spread through the whole school. I overhear a bunch of Year 10 girls talking about it in the canteen.

"He seems really nice though!"

"I don't know, I always thought there was something weird about him."

"He doesn't look like a perv."

"You can't tell who's a perv and who isn't just by looking."

"It's probably bollocks. But I'm keeping my distance, just to be on the safe side."

Where the hell did this come from? I don't have anything about Mr. Ackerly on my phone. Obviously Mimi has it in for him, but there's no way of knowing whether he actually did something dodgy – to her or to someone she cares about – or just gave her crappy grades. If it's the latter, perhaps Mimi is in my Drama class.

With this in mind, I get to Drama class early on Monday morning and watch everyone file in, comparing each of them to the blurry picture of Mimi I've built up in my head. I lean against the wall, unsure of what to do with my hands since I don't have my phone to fiddle with. I had caved and told Mum I'd lost it, so she let me borrow the ancient one she uses as an alarm clock. I can't do anything on it, not even check Twitter or play one measly game of Candy Crush. It's like living in the 1950s.

When Bonnie arrives, she comes up to me and says, "Brace yourself; we've got Mrs. Dixon today."

Mrs. Dixon is an old hippy who smells like herbal tea. She likes making Drama students pretend to be trees, and every so often she makes me promise never to stop painting, even though I quit Art after Year 9 and haven't painted anything other than my nails since then. I think she has me confused with someone else.

"Why Mrs. Dixon? Is Mr. Ackerly not here?"

"I don't know. He was here this morning but he didn't look well. I walked past the staff room and he was all hunched over and pale."

"Maybe it's the stress," I say, assuming Bonnie will know what I'm talking about. She does.

"Do you think he'll get fired?" she asks, her eyes shining with something like excitement. "I mean, I know it's just an anonymous comment on Facebook, but as soon as people's parents hear about it there's gonna be complaints."

Wait a minute. Is Mimi Bonnie? She's got a track record of getting involved with older men – what if one of those older men was Mr. Ackerly? I decide to test the waters.

"I don't know, but it'd suck if he did get fired. We'd probably get stuck with Mrs. Dixon for the rest of the year."

"Yeah, but don't you care that he might try and grope you? Or worse?"

I think of his hand on the small of my back in the props cupboard and realise that I do care. I care very much. But I push on regardless, needing to see how Bonnie reacts. "There's no evidence that he did anything. Anyone can post an anonymous comment."

"You can't just dismiss it, though. There's no smoke without fire."

"There's plenty of smoke without fire. Smoke machines, cigarettes, burnt toast–"

"Everything's a joke to you, isn't it?" she interrupts. Her face is flushed and there's a sharp vertical line between her eyebrows. I ought to shut up, but I'm not going to. She looks so agitated, I really feel like she might know more about this whole shebang than she's letting on. And whatever she knows, I want to know.

"Look, no offence but I wouldn't have thought you'd be all that bothered. I mean, your boyfriend's twenty-six and Mr. Ackerly can't be much older than that. So what's the difference?"

She pauses, turns even pinker, then looks at me very directly and says, "The difference between being touched when you want to be touched, and being touched when you don't want to be touched is *everything*."

Mrs. Dixon bursts in, carrying a bushel of scripts and some kind of Native American headdress, and Bonnie moves away from me. She doesn't look at me for the rest of the class.

It's a Wednesday morning. Mimi hasn't posted anything since her post about Mr. Ackerly, so it looks like she's done. She's left a hell of a mess behind, which was presumably just what she wanted. Her mischief has left a lingering, prickly tension in the air, and I've not seen hide nor hair of Mr. Ackerly.

We have a Sixth Form assembly in the hall, which is already overheated and stuffy. It'll be worse by lunchtime. I sit down in my plastic chair, wishing I was done with all this. Assemblies, school dinners, these fucking plastic chairs with no lower back support, everything. I want to get on a train, fall asleep, and wake up somewhere far, far away. Amongst all the chatter and scraping of chair legs I hear someone behind me yawn, obnoxiously loud.

Ms. Greenwood (head of Sixth Form) strides onto the little stage at the front of the hall. Her heels make a lot of noise on the wooden floor. Important-sounding shoes. I'd get myself a pair that sounded like that, if I could run in them. She clears her throat into the microphone at the front of the stage, and the dull roar of noise that fills the hall subsides, slowly and grudgingly.

"Today I'd like to talk to you about cyberbullying." And just like that, Ms. Greenwood has everyone's attention. "So what exactly do I mean by cyberbullying?"

Nobody says anything, assuming it's a rhetorical question. But Ms. Greenwood waits for an answer and the silence in the hall seems to get thicker and thicker, until it's like a weight on my chest and I can't stand it anymore. "Online bullying!" I call out, cringing a little at the sound of my own voice.

"That's right. Bullying someone online by posting or sending unpleasant messages, usually anonymously. Now, the content of these messages can be anything. For example, did you know that 19 percent of cyberbullying involves spreading rumors about the victim?"

If there was any doubt before, there certainly isn't now. This assembly is about Mimi. Fat lot of good it's going to do. She's stopped posting now, and no-one can undo what she already did. Also, where was this assembly when she first started doing her thing? Teachers don't care when it's students getting dragged through the mud; they only care when a teacher's name gets mucky. I try to focus on this, try to stay pissed off instead of feeling sickeningly guilty.

I listen to Ms. Greenwood spouting statistics about cyberbullying, watch the video she plays about some girl who got cyberbullied and topped herself, and I sweat buckets.

The assembly seems to go on forever, but finally Ms. Greenwood wraps things up with "So let's all put a little more thought into what we post online. Because you never know what the consequences might be," and there is a silence made of pure awkwardness.

"Okay, now for a couple of announcements," she says briskly, and for the first time since the beginning of the assembly, I feel like I can breathe easily. The first announcement, however, almost stops me breathing all together. "We've had a phone handed in to lost property. It's a Samsung 4G and the cover has a picture of a lizard in a trench coat and a hat."

A lizard in a trench coat and a hat. Detective Gecko. My phone. The prospect of finally getting my phone back ought to have me sobbing with relief, but I really wish she hadn't announced that in front of everyone, after an assembly that was obviously all about Mimi. I don't want anyone figuring out the connection between my phone and Mimi's mischief. Dave Halliday, in the row in front of me, cranes his neck round to look at me and I pretend not to notice him. He knows it's my phone. Nobody else in this school has a Detective Gecko phone case, and I used to think that was a good thing. I used to think it was good to stand out rather than blend in. *What an idiot.*

the heist

chapter thirteen

I have very mixed feelings about my phone at the moment. That isn't something I ever expected, because I used to love my phone with all my rotten little heart. Now, it's more complicated. On the one hand, I need it back, like, right now. On the other hand, I don't exactly want it. It's been spoiled, somehow.

Since Mimi managed to hack into it, the password protection is probably gone. That means anyone could have seen my carefully labelled files of information. The person who found the phone, for example, or Mrs. Kayani, the receptionist. What if the person who found the phone dug through all the files in horrified fascination and now thinks it belongs to Mimi? What if Mrs. Kayani had a nosy peek at the phone's contents, got concerned at what she found, and told a teacher? Or teachers, plural? Or any member of staff who'd listen?

I feel paranoid and permanently tense. Maybe I wouldn't make a very good spy after all. How did Lana Barrington deal with the fear of being caught out? Alcohol, I think. She drank a lot of gimlets, whatever they are.

In Geography, while I'm supposed to be learning about glaciers, I formulate a plan. I need to get my phone back, but I mustn't let anyone see me doing this. No good just walking up to Reception and asking for it. I'll have to get it back discreetly, then take the cover off so it looks like any other phone, and put the password protection back in place. Then I'll just keep my head down and wait for all this to blow over.

By lunchtime, I've sweat so much from the anxiety that I must be starting to stink. This, of course, stresses me out further and makes me sweat even more. Time to get this over with.

At Birchwood, lost property is kept in the little office behind the Reception desk. The only obstacle in the way is Mrs. Kayani. She's the mum of Salim Kayani (I sat next to him in History last year); everyone knows that. What everyone doesn't know is that she lives in constant fear of Salim's allergies, which cover everything from bee stings to shellfish. I found this out during my snooping and it didn't seem particularly interesting at the time, but that's the thing – you never know when a piece of information will come in handy.

Now I just need to find a messenger. There are people milling about everywhere in front of Reception. Girls sitting on the wide steps leading up to the building, stretched out with their skirts hitched up to get a better tan. Kids sat on the grassy area to the left, in the shade of that tree with the white blossom that inexplicably smells like feet. Two boys throwing clumps of just-mown grass at each other.

I set my sights on Brianna Richardson. She's the younger sister of Edie Richardson – her with the kink about the smell of fresh washing. I've spoken to her a few times because I used to go round Edie's house a lot in Year 10, and a bit in Year 11, so I'm not a total stranger to her. Also, I don't have to worry about her mentioning this to Edie because the two of them hardly speak to each other. Edie is embarrassed by her sister's existence. Brianna sits on the steps, tucked away on the right so that she's half in the shade and half in the sun. She's on her own and on her phone. Judging by the way her thumbs are moving, she's playing a game.

"Hey, Brianna."

She pauses the game and looks up. Like her sister, she's ginger. Actually, no. Edie's not ginger, she's a redhead, and that's different. Redheads are sexy, in a fiery kind of way. Gingers are just ginger. I'm not sure what the difference is, but I think it's less to do with the exact shade of your hair and more to do with the rest of you. Like, if you have flawless skin, full lips and an hourglass figure, you're a redhead. If you have braces, spots and a flat chest, you're a ginger.

"Hey..." she says, and squints like she's trying to remember my name.

"Gwen."

"Oh yeah. Sorry, you look different."

"Yep, new hair. Um, could you do me a massive favor?"

"Depends what it is."

She's got this guarded look about her, and I'm getting worried that she is not the same guileless girl I remember. She must be fourteen or fifteen now. She's probably grown out of her pony phase.

"It'll only take a minute. Could you go and tell Mrs. Kayani that her son's in the nurse's office because he's had an allergic reaction. He's okay, it's not serious, but he's asking for her."

"Why don't you tell her?"

"Because... it's kind of my fault that he had an allergic reaction."

"What did you do?"

"Just gave him a bite of my sandwich."

"What was in it?"

"Something that's given him big red hives all over the place. So I'd rather not face the wrath of an angry mum – you understand, right?"

"Yeah."

"Thanks, hon, you're a star."

Brianna smiles at that, gets up, and trots up the stairs and into Reception. I steal her place at the side of the steps, out of the way, until Mrs. Kayani comes rushing out in a flurry of maternal anxiety. Then I slip into Reception before Brianna can ask any questions.

Past the big desk and into the little office behind it. Thank God it's unlocked. I close the door behind me, doing a quick and sloppy mental calculation of how much time I have. I turn to face the room, which looks so much like a badly-organised jumble sale that my heart sinks. Why is there so much crap? Do they never throw anything out? Cardboard box full of jumpers, another full of umbrellas. Gloves, headphones, a Rimmel lipstick, a copy of *The Fault in Our Stars*, a shoebox full of mobile phones, a couple of pencil cases, a purple hat… wait, rewind a bit.

I grab the shoebox with the mobile phones and find mine instantly. There's only one other modern phone in the box. The rest all look really old – a couple of them even have buttons. I slip my phone into the pocket of my trousers, then pause at the door of the little office. I listen to make sure I can't hear anyone, then arrange my face into a neutral, casual expression, and open the door.

It's not so easy to keep the neutral, casual expression intact as I leave Reception, feeling like I have a pocketful of stolen diamonds. A little bit of that old buzz reappears – the buzz I used to get from filling up this phone with secrets – but it's not the same. Mimi screwed it all up.

I rush down the steps and head towards the Mistory block (A building that contains the Maths and History classrooms. That's not its official name, it's just what everyone calls it). I go straight to the toilets, lock myself in a cubicle, and pull my phone out of my pocket. My palms are so sweaty, the damn thing almost slips out of my hand and into the toilet.

The first thing I do is take the Detective Gecko cover off. The second thing I do is try switching it on, wondering if it has any battery. It does. Weirdly, the password protection is still intact. Everything looks the same. The phone doesn't feel like it's been hacked into, even though it obviously has (my password is not the guessable kind), and that's pretty disturbing. I put the phone back in my pocket, lean against the wall of the cubicle, and just breathe for a moment. Long, slow breaths, which do fuck all to calm me down.

movie night

chapter fourteen

Once I have my phone back, I try my best to forget about Mimi and Mr. Ackerly and everything that's been going on. I go straight home from school. Part of me actually wishes I had some homework or revision to do, but AS levels are over and school is mostly a doss at this point. I feed the hens their dinner. I eat my own dinner.

Needing the distraction of company, I type out a hesitant message to Ethan, asking if he wants to come over and watch a movie. Then I remember that he has no interest in being "friend-zoned" so why the hell would he be interested in coming over to watch a movie with no chance of making out or getting his bits touched? I consider deleting the message, but then I send it anyway. It's just one evening. Just one movie, then we can go back to not talking if that's what he wants. The worst he can do is say no.

Half an hour later, Ethan turns up at the front door with a large bag of Tangy Cheese Doritos and an awkward grin. I hug him impulsively, and he hugs me back tightly with one arm. The hug lingers and the Doritos get crushed between us.

"So, what are we watching?" he asks as he steps inside. "And where are we watching it?"

"Well, Mum and Dad are watching *The Great British Bake Off* in the living room, but I'm gonna see if I can persuade them to watch it upstairs."

Ethan follows me towards the living room, but stands hesitantly in the doorway as I perch on the arm of the sofa, next to Mum.

"How's bread week?"

"We're at a bit of a crisis point actually – Susan's blackberry jam has gone missing."

"Oh, no! Me and Ethan are going upstairs to watch a movie. Let me know how it turns out, with the jam."

Mum and Dad both tear their eyes away from the screen and stare at Ethan, who points at the TV and says, "I bet Nick's stolen it. He's had it in for Susan since week two."

"Ethan, good to see you, mate," says Dad. His voice doesn't match the words he is saying. He sounds unusually stern.

"Gwen, you didn't mention Ethan was coming over," says Mum, turning to give me an accusatory glare.

"It was kind of a spur-of-the-moment thing. And we're not going to bother you, we're just going to watch a movie in my bedroom."

At this point, Mum and Dad look at each other and have one of those conversations that they have sometimes, which are made up entirely of facial expressions and vague gestures. After a couple of seconds, Dad says, "We'll watch the rest of *Bake Off* upstairs. You can have the big telly."

"Really? Thanks!" I exclaim, fake-surprised like this wasn't exactly what I had intended.

With Mum and Dad gone, me and Ethan settle down on the sofa. We are both in the mood for a Marvel movie, and spend a good five minutes debating which ones are good and which ones aren't before settling on the second Captain America. We sit close together, but not touching, and pass the bag of Doritos back and forth, getting orange dust all over our fingers. I wonder, for the third or fourth time, why I don't feel the slightest fluttering of desire for Chris Evans. The guy is all muscles and eyelashes, which must be a killer combination because Martine and Angie both fancy the pants off him and they usually have different types.

"If you could have any superpower, what would you pick?" says Ethan.

I chew this over. A few weeks ago, I would have picked invisibility in a heartbeat – all the better for spying. Now, I think I'd still choose it, but for slightly different reasons. It'd be good for avoiding trouble.

"I'd probably pick invisibility."

"And sneak into the boys' changing rooms?"

"Why would I waste a superpower on that? It's not exactly difficult to see naked people, they're all over the internet."

"Yes, I'm aware." Ethan's voice is dry and a corner of his mouth quirks into a knowing smile. Time to get the subject back on track.

"So, what would you pick?" I ask.

"Shape-shifting."

"Really? I thought you'd pick flying."

"I could shape-shift into a bird."

"What about invisibility?"

"I could shape-shift into a table and no-one would know I was there."

"Super-strength?"

"Boring."

"Mind control?"

"Only manipulators pick mind control."

I'm giggling now, feeling more relaxed than I have in ages. I love the way his brain works, and I think about telling him this but decide not to, in case it sounds creepy. Too intimate, complimenting someone on their thought processes. Safer to stick with external stuff like clothes and hair.

To compensate for not being able to say the stupid shit I want to say, I cuddle up to him and rest my head on his shoulder. He's warm, and surprisingly comfortable, and all the drama of the past few weeks fades away into insignificance. All is right with the world, until—

"Gwen, you're kind of giving me some mixed signals here."

"Hm?" He turns his head to look down at me but I can't see him properly; our faces are too close together. I pull away from him. "What do you mean?"

"The last conversation we had, you basically said that you didn't want to go out. Then you invite me over to watch a film and you're kind of... coming on to me."

"What the hell? How am I coming on to you?" My voice rises in irritation, but then I remember Mum and Dad upstairs and hush myself up quickly.

"By being all cuddly!"

"I haven't done anything to you that I wouldn't do to a female friend or my bloody *parents*!"

"You know it's different when you're with a bloke. I just wish you'd be more clear with me, like, can't you just tell me what you want?"

Well, fuck. What do I want, exactly? "Why don't you just tell me what *you* want?"

A pause. Ethan doesn't answer the big questions flippantly, but neither does he leave them unanswered. "I want more."

"Like, more of this? To spend more time with me? Watch more movies together and have more conversations that seem really childish but are actually kind of thought-provoking?"

"Well, yes, all of that."

"I want that too." My eyes are stinging, because I wish more than anything that we could leave the conversation there. "But I don't think you really want *more*. I think you want *different*."

Ethan says nothing for a long moment. I turn back to the TV, where there is a big fight scene going on. Slick and choreographed and brutal. My stomach aches.

"When you said the friend-zone is the only zone you have," says Ethan, "was that just an excuse so I wouldn't feel bad, or did you mean it?"

"I meant it."

"I don't get it. Do your parents not want you having boyfriends yet?"

"No, that's not it."

"Do you maybe... do you maybe like girls? Because you know that's totally okay, right, you know I'd understand."

"No, I don't like girls. And you know what, I'm starting to not like you either. Why can't you just leave it alone?"

Oh crap. Puffer-fish mode. I've gone all spiky so he can't get to me.

"Maybe I should go."

"Yeah, maybe you should."

"Fine, then."

He stands up slowly, then walks towards the door of the living room slowly, like he's expecting me to stop him.

I could stop him, but what then? He wants one of two things from me:

1) A girlfriend-boyfriend relationship, or

2) An explanation as to why he can't have that.

I can't give him either of those things, so I say nothing and let him leave.

found out

chapter fifteen

It's Thursday, and I'm twenty minutes into Spanish class when I catch Jodi Tustin whispering something to Kelly Kowalski, then looking at me with an expression that's not quite a scowl, but worse than a frown.

I try to ignore the little spike of panic. Try to tell myself it's like an aftershock. A bit of lingering paranoia. But then I remember the photos I took in Jodi's bedroom, and Mimi posting them on Facebook, and Jodi walking in on me fake-sleeping on her bed. I'd better stay away from Jodi. I'd better stay away from everyone.

To this end, I eat lunch by myself in a corner of the canteen, keeping my eyes on my food. Today it is some kind of unidentifiable fish with cheese sauce. Angie used to say that the cheese sauce from the canteen tastes like cum, which made me feel weird for liking it. I just like salty food, is all. Usually I'd be eating lunch with whoever, trying to get information out of them – you can make the most probing questions sound casual while you've got a mouthful of food. Or I'd be sitting as close as possible to an interesting conversation, taking mental notes to translate later into actual notes. But I'm done with all that now. I'm done trying to understand people.

My phone buzzes, and when I whip it out there's a message from Jodi. It says "Hi." That's all. I stare at the word in confusion for a moment, then look up and see Jodi standing right there, across the table from me.

Kelly Kowalski is with her too. Jodi says, "Can I borrow your phone really quickly? It's an emergency." Without waiting for a reply, she snatches my phone, and I'm too gobsmacked to stop her.

She's looking at my phone. She's going to see all my files. She's going to see her own name and find the photos I took in her bedroom. She's going to think I'm Mimi. The ground shifts under me and my stomach lurches, seasick. I stand up and make a grab for my phone but the table is between me and Jodi and all she has to do to avoid me is take a neat half-step back. I try to go around the table but Kelly stands very deliberately in the way, hands on her broad hips. The scuffle has attracted attention, and people are staring. Desperately, I push past Kelly and grab my phone. It's too late. I can tell from Jodi's face that she's seen enough.

I'm expecting a slap in the face. I'm expecting Jodi to

start yelling at me, making loud, sweary accusations for everyone to hear. What actually happens is way worse. Jodi gives me a look that starts out angry, then morphs into something more complex. There's disgust in there, I think. Maybe confusion. Very quietly, she says, "What the fuck is wrong with you?" and waits for a couple of seconds, like she's actually expecting an answer. I've got nothing. She turns around and walks away. Kelly follows, looking daggers at me as she passes. More than daggers, actually. Swords and axes and bullets and poison.

On the bus, on the way home, I have a crazy idea. I could tell Mum or Dad what's going on. I could tell them everything, right from the beginning. I'd have to figure out where the beginning is, of course, but I reckon I could do that if I tried. Maybe they could give me some advice. Maybe they could drag me out of this hole I've dug myself into.

When I get home, Mum is already back from work and she's in the kitchen, making angry bread. Mum doesn't like cooking much but she does like making bread, and she makes two kinds. One is angry bread, and she makes this by attacking the dough like it's a punch bag. The other kind of bread is made more slowly. She kneads the dough to a rhythm, folding and squeezing, folding and squeezing. She gets this soft, day-dreamy look.

"Bad day?" I ask, as I stand at the kitchen sink and pour myself a glass of water.

"Exceptionally bad," she says, slapping the dough against the table for emphasis. "I said I had a migraine and left early."

"Naughty."

There's a grim smile on Mum's face. "Tilly doesn't believe in migraines." Tilly is her boss, and a general pain in the arse. "She thinks it's just someone making a fuss about a headache. So I specifically chose a migraine, just to annoy her."

"Can I have some of that?" I gesture at the lump of dough with my pinkie finger.

"Tie your hair up first."

I drink a few mouthfuls of water, then take a rubber band from the rubber band jar on the windowsill (the rubber band jar is between the swear jar and the button jar – this family goes through a lot of jam and Mum doesn't like to throw away the jars, which is probably something to do with growing up broke.) I scrape back my hair and tie it into a bun, then rinse my hands under the hot tap and dry them on a tea towel.

Mum tears the dough and gives me a generous half. I smack down into the warm squishiness with the heel of my hand and instantly feel a tiny bit better. I knead until my arms ache, throwing all my weight into it. Throwing everything I have into it. Me and Mum beat up our wads of dough in unison, and we don't talk about our shitty days. For the first time in my life, I feel like me and Mum are actually quite similar.

polygraph

Lana's father was mad at her. His eyes were bulging and his face was red. "I oughta belt your behind until there's no skin left on it," he said, and Lana put her hands over her buttocks protectively. Why was he so angry? She must have done something stupid, because when she was bad he only got a little mad, but when she was stupid he got furious. Keeping her distance from him, Lana watched her father age and sicken very rapidly, then shrink and turn into a gravestone. At the same time, Lana shot up and was no longer a child.

She was awake now, but still did not feel fully conscious. With great difficulty, she pulled herself up off the floor and into a sitting position. Her legs refused to move in the way she wanted them to, so they ended up sticking out at uncomfortable angles. They had drugged her; she was sure of it. They must have put something in the thin stew they had brought her last night. Her head seemed to be quite separate from her body, floating a few inches above her neck. She sincerely hoped this was due to the drugs and not some kind of premonition.

A small quantity of watery light leaked through the tiny barred window in the door of the cell. It must be dawn, or just after. Lana looked around the narrow room, with its narrow bed, and for a moment she could not recall why she had chosen to sleep on the floor, squashed between the metal bed frame and the wall. Then she took a good look at the mattress and saw those rust-coloured stains.

She had to stop looking at the bloodstains on the mattress. They did not frighten her much, but they distracted her. Whenever she saw them, she started to wonder who had occupied this cell before her, and what that person's eventual fate had been. She could not afford that kind of distraction when she needed to focus on her own sorry plight and wiggling out of it as soon as she could.

Footsteps sounded in the hall outside the cell. Lana tried to tense her muscles in preparation for whatever was about to happen, but her whole body felt rubbery and soft. She managed to pull herself to her feet and stand up straight, just as the door opened. The face in the doorway was familiar. The man it belonged to had been wearing a camel-coloured coat last time, but now he was in a grey uniform. The colour of storm clouds, Lana thought as she looked him up and down. She wasn't apt to get poetic at a time like this, or any time really. Perhaps it was the drugs.

"Come with me," said the guard, reaching out for her.

"To where?" said Lana, in German, as she took a clumsy step backwards.

"To a larger room."

She couldn't fight him off, especially in her current state, and the prospect of a little more space to stretch out in was so appealing that Lana decided to follow him without a fuss. Holding her elbow in a way that must have looked gentlemanly but would certainly leave bruises, he led her down the dismal, echoing corridor, past a number of identical doors with tiny, barred windows set into them. A face peered from one of these windows, and for a moment Lana felt absurdly self-conscious about her shapeless prisoner's smock. They had taken her pearls, of course, before she even had a chance to think about biting down on the one filled with cyanide. At the end of the corridor was a flight of stairs, which Lana climbed with great difficulty.

"What did they put in the stew?" Lana asked the guard.

"Meat and vegetables."

"You seem to have a habit of answering the wrong part of the question."

"I don't understand you. Perhaps your German is not as good as you think."

At the top of the staircase was another corridor; better lit than the one below, and lacking that sharp, bitter stink that Lana hadn't been able to identify. The guard brought her to a door, which he knocked on sharply, and opened when a cheerful-sounding voice beyond it gave him permission to do so. He shoved Lana roughly into the room, making her stumble.

The room was harshly-lit, and the light bounced off white tiles, like the kind in a public restroom. There were two people there, besides Lana and the guard. One was a small, balding, round-faced man in spectacles, seated at a square desk with some kind of box-shaped, scientific-looking instrument on top of it. The other man was younger, taller and blonder. He looked wiry, though it was difficult to tell. Lana always resented the fact that a man's clothes gave so very little away about the body underneath them. Not like women's clothes, which clung to every shapely curve or unsightly bulge. And of course, so many men wore uniforms these days. These two had white coats, which made a change from the SS uniforms, but gave Lana the uncomfortable feeling that she was about to become a lab rat.

"That will be all, thank you. You can leave her here," said the round-faced man, and the guard left the room, closing the door behind him. "Please, sit down," the round-faced man continued, indicating a chair on the opposite side of his desk. "My name is Doctor Richter and my assistant here is Mr. Scholz."

Lana glanced at Scholz where he leaned impassively against the wall of the room, with a clipboard dangling from one hand. She took the chair opposite Richter, and when she sat down to face him she found him smiling gently. It was the first time anyone had smiled at her in a long time.

"Now, Mr. Scholz will only be observing," Richter continued, "so long as you cooperate. Do you understand?"

"Perfectly."

Lana had meant to use a colder voice, but there was something disarming about Richter's small smile and pleasant manner. Besides, the drugs still hadn't worn off, so she had much less fight in her than usual. She was compliant as a rag doll while Richter attached her to the strange apparatus on the desk, explaining it to her in the tone of voice used by schoolmarms for teaching arithmetic to slow children.

"This is called a polygraph," he said. "Also known as a lie detector. There's no need to worry; it won't hurt you. What it does is measure certain physiological changes that happen when we tell lies. We will ask you some questions, and the machine will show us whether or not you are telling the truth."

These things don't work, Lana told herself. A machine can't read a person's mind – it's only meant to scare people into confessions. She almost managed to convince herself.

"Let's begin," said Richter, settling himself at the desk. "Please answer the following questions honestly, unless I say otherwise. What month is it?"

"October."

"How many people are in this room?"

"Three."

"What is my name?"

"Doctor Richter."

As Lana answered these inane questions, a pen attached to the polygraph machine by a thin metal arm began to draw a line on a long sheet of paper. The line showed a number of peaks and troughs, but only small ones.

"Very good. Now, for this next question, I want you to

answer with a lie. What colour tie am I wearing?"

"Pink."

"There, you see? The machine shows that you are lying." Lana stared at the sheet of paper in curiosity, and then dismay. The peaks and troughs drawn by the pen had clearly grown. "Now, let's begin in earnest, shall we? Is your name Ingrid Pfeiffer?"

"Yes." The peaks and troughs on the paper were small and neat. The machine believed her, and why shouldn't it? That was what almost everyone had called her for almost six months. Like all her pseudonyms, she was at ease with it.

"Is your name Lana Barrington?"

Lana hadn't been expecting that, but she wasn't overly surprised. "Yes."

Once again, the machine proclaimed her honesty. Richter tilted his head to the side with an expression of mild interest. "Is your name Marie Boucher?"

"Yes."

"Is your name Alma Jones?"

"Yes."

He might know all her pseudonyms, but Lana was damned if she'd let him know which was her real name. She kept her breathing slow and even and watched Richter watching the pen slide across the paper. "Very interesting," he said quietly, then looked up and smiled at her. This was not the polite smile he had given her a few minutes ago, but a strange, gleeful grin that seemed to contain a remarkable number of teeth. It was a shark's smile in a teddy bear's face.

"So, Ingrid, you are the woman of a thousand names."

"That's very poetic. For a scientist."

"I think you'll find, Lana, that poets and scientists are much the same. We are both simply trying to understand the world and everything in it. But let's not waste time on philosophy. Let's talk about you instead."

"Wonderful. Most dates I go on, the man wants to talk about himself all night."

"Then I think you will find me a charming companion."

"I have no doubt. But this place lacks a romantic atmosphere."

Richter smiled. Not his alarming grin of delight, but his polite, indulgent smirk. He picked up a file next to the polygraph, opened it and perused it. "So, Marie," he began, not taking his eyes off the file, "I see you have been employed by the French Resistance. And the Office of Strategic Services. And even, very briefly, by us."

Lana said nothing.

"Tell me, Alma, where were you born?"

"In a bathtub. It's a long story. A funny story, if you're hearing it for the first time."

"How old are you?"

"I'm a lady. I don't answer any questions with a numerical answer."

"Where did you learn to speak German?"

"I'm good with languages."

Richter closed the file and put it down. He leaned back in his chair and crossed his arms across his chest, looking relaxed and thoughtful. "A woman with several different names, shifting allegiances, and an inability to answer the simplest questions about herself," he mused, sounding as though he were talking to himself rather than talking to Lana. "I think there are two possibilities."

"And those are?"

"Either you have a very complicated plan, or you have nothing. No roots, no moral compass, no idea of who you are..."

"I know exactly who I am," Lana snapped, suddenly angry.

Richter stared at the polygraph. Seething, Lana followed his gaze. According to that damn machine, she was lying.

whoops, I broke everything

chapter sixteen

In one of the fields near my house, there's a flock of sheep that graze there from time to time. If you walk through the field, they all stare at you in a very Alfred Hitchcock way, and if you get too close, they all turn and run simultaneously. Honestly, I kind of like it. It makes me feel dangerous, like a wolf or something. It's not so much fun when people look at you like that, though. Or when people turn and walk away as soon as you get near them.

It's almost the summer holidays. Mr. Ackerly is nowhere to be seen. I am a social pariah. Word got out that Mimi = Gwen, and it spread as quickly as any half-decent half-lie. Girls look at me and whisper to each other pointedly. In Spanish class, someone wrote "Acosador" on a sticker and stuck it to the back of my chair. According to Google Translate, this is Spanish for "Stalker". Of course, not everyone has the capacity for foreign insults, so there is a fair amount of primary school stuff going on. Ralph Davies, for example, stuck his foot out as I was walking past him, so that I tripped over it. I should have fallen. Pretended to be badly hurt. Turned it back around on him. Instead, I just stumbled and flailed my arms about embarrassingly.

When I was a kid, if anyone picked on me, Mum would tell me to rise above it. "Don't stoop to their level," she'd say, "because you're better than that." Well, there's no rising above this. I'm already on their level. Way below it, in fact. People look at me like I'm a slug or a goose turd or something. That's pretty much how I feel.

It's bad enough during and between lessons, but lunchtimes are the worst. Nobody wants to sit with me, let alone talk to me. Eating alone in a little circle of emptiness, in the middle of a very crowded canteen, has got to be one of the loneliest feelings in the world. I've taken to bringing sandwiches and eating them in the computer room, like the socially awkward thirteen-year-old boys who spend their lunchtimes playing endless Fortnite.

On the very last day of school, I log in to Facebook and am not remotely surprised to find that there's now a page exclusively dedicated to posting made-up crap about me. A lot of it is sexual. Things like "Gwen gives head behind the bike sheds" and "Gwen dyed her pubes black so that the carpet matches the curtains" and "Gwen fingered herself with a Mars Bar." The last one in particular pisses me off, because it doesn't even make sense. How is it fingering yourself if you use anything other than your fingers? And why would anyone do that with a Mars Bar? Messy, and a waste of chocolate. I wrap up my sandwiches, which I have no appetite for anymore. I decide to skip my afternoon classes, go home, and start the summer holidays early.

On the bus, the bitter-tasting lump that seems to be permanently lodged in my throat starts to swell, and threatens to squeeze tears out of my eyes. I try to focus on other things, like what the fuck I'm going to do all summer. Maybe I should get a job. Maybe I should help Dad build a new chicken run for the hens – something 100 percent fox-proof, with seven-foot fences and a foot of chicken wire underground so nothing can dig underneath it. He started talking about that a few weeks ago and I offered to help him, but then the shit hit the fan and I totally forgot about it.

Yeah, that's what I'll do. I'll build a new chicken run. I'll volunteer at the stables, mucking out and grooming the horses. I'll spend this summer around animals and stay well away from people.

When I get home, I make myself a coffee, slip into my wellies, and go straight into the garden. The sunshine is dazzling, the sky is marbled blue and white, and the smell of my coffee disguises the other smell in the garden. But only for a moment. When my nose catches that metallic tang on the air, I set my mug on the ground and by the time

I straighten up again, I'm shaking. My body reacts to the smell of blood before my brain does.

I walk down the garden, towards the chicken run. There's a scraped patch of earth where something – I already know exactly what something – has dug under the fence. There's a dark smear of blood on the dirt.

With my hands cupped over my nose and mouth to block out the smell, I go into the run. Feathers on the ground. I'm praying silently. Not to God, but to the fox. Please, tell me you only took one of them. Please, leave me something.

The inside of the henhouse is a horror movie. Feathers are pasted to the walls with blood. More feathers on the floor, like a blanket of dirty snow. Marjory, Helen, and June are corpses. Susie is gone.

My ears are ringing. I'm going to faint. I stumble away from the henhouse, sit down heavily and put my head on my knees. It doesn't help. The world is still spinning and fuzzy-edged. I shuffle around, lie down on the ground and prop my feet up against the henhouse. I'm probably lying in feathers or chicken shit or chicken blood, but I'm past caring.

As my own blood flows down from my propped-up feet to my failing brain, the dizziness finally subsides. I'm clammy with sweat and starting to feel cold despite the summer heat. I start crying. Since I'm lying down, the tears fall sideways and get into my ears. The hens are dead. Everything is broken. I've broken everything.

darren

I haven't thought much about Darren lately. I don't like to think about people when they aren't around.

My brother is two years and ten months older than me, and never lets me forget it. He thinks he knows everything, which he doesn't, but I have to admit that he does know a lot. He reads books on geotechnical engineering for fun, and intends to be rich one day. We disagree about pretty much everything. He's never given Mum and Dad any trouble because he doesn't like to drink and he could never get the kind of girls that Mum would hate. He has a sense of humour, though it usually only appears when he's being mean. When he's being mean, I'm usually the target. This is the guy who found me crying on the ground in the chicken run.

Darren looks down at me, then over to the henhouse, then back at me and he says, "Fox?"

"Yeah," I say, and my voice comes out as a croak.

"Did you faint?"

"No."

He looks sceptical about this. He reaches out both hands and when I grab them he pulls me to my feet. I stumble, but he steadies me. "There's blood on your neck," he says, so I wipe the side of my neck. Now there's blood on my hand.

In the bathroom, I sit on the toilet seat while Darren runs me a bath. He dumps about half the bottle of Dad's Radox for Men in it – there will be bubbles up to the ceiling and Dad will be annoyed and I will smell all peppery, like Dad. But it's a kind gesture.

In exchange for the kind gesture, I try to talk even though I really don't want to. "How's uni?" I ask, my voice still thick from crying.

"Yeah, good. How's things with you? Apart from just now, I mean." I shrug. "School okay?" I shrug again. "Got a boyfriend yet?"

"Ugh," I say, letting the disgust show on my face because I'm suddenly very tired and exhaustion makes me honest.

Darren is silent for a long moment. Then he turns off the tap and says, "I've missed your scintillating conversation." He leaves me alone in the bathroom, taking a stray chicken feather out of my hair as he passes.

I lock the bathroom door, then strip my clothes off slowly and clumsily, and step into the bath. The water is too hot but I don't care. I will stay here getting cooked, like a lump of meat in a stew, until I feel less raw.

dream girl

chapter seventeen

I haven't left the house in three days. Normally, after three days cooped up inside I'd be going stir-crazy. Itching and twitching with the need for something, anything, to happen. I used to hate being bored, but these days I quite like it. I feel fine. Well, maybe fine isn't the right word. Numb. That's it. Mum is worried about me because I'm not eating much or talking much or doing much. She keeps going on about summer job opportunities on local farms, but I tune her out. I can't seem to do anything more productive than watch telly, but I do manage to read a few chapters of *Dead Tulips*. Maybe that's why I dream of Lana Barrington.

We are sitting next to each other on a park bench. She has a gun in her lap and a gunshot wound in her chest, slowly oozing blood. Also, her hands are made of sausages.

I am smoking a cigarette, which is something I've never done in real life.

"What am I doing here?" Lana Barrington asks, glancing down at the bullet hole in her chest and looking pissed off.

"I dunno."

"You asked me to come."

"Did I? Sorry."

She makes a disgruntled noise and sparks up a cigarette of her own. Clumsily, because of her sausage hands. She inhales the smoke and it oozes out of the hole in her chest.

"So, do you want to be me or be with me?" she asks. "Or is it a bit of both?"

"I think it's a bit of neither," I say.

I take a drag of my cigarette and when I exhale, the words come out like smoke through my pursed lips.

"I suppose I just wanted to think there was someone out there like me. Way cooler than me, but, y'know. Someone who feels the same things. And doesn't feel the same things. Someone who'd understand. You understand, right?"

"Of course I do, doll. But I'm not real."

a night out

Now I haven't left the house in five days and I still feel numb as a frostbitten finger. It would probably worry me if I were capable of feeling worried. I've decided to go out tonight.

At 7pm, I change out of my PJs and into tight black jeans and an equally-tight black top. I do my make-up, slicking up my lips with the bright red Kiss of Death lipstick. I stopped wearing it during all that Mimi business, but tonight I want red lips. I'm going to get drunk tonight, and I'm going to talk to strangers, and I might even let one of them take me home, if they ask. Maybe that's a bad idea, but I want to feel something. Anything.

The bus into town is still hot from a day of fierce sunshine, and it smells of sweat. Not B.O., just sweat. It's not such a bad smell, really. If I close my eyes and breathe in slowly and think of sweat-damp skin moving over sweat-damp skin, I can feel stuff happening downstairs. I've understood this for a while – my body works normally; it's my brain that's wired wrong.

It's too early to go to a club, so I go to The Tipsy Sparrow. It's a decent pub, though it's not as cute as its name would suggest. I go straight up to the bar and wait for a burly guy with tattooed arms to collect his four pints and try to carry them back to his table all at once.

"What can I get you?" asks the barmaid, who has a nose ring and epic cleavage. My tits feel suddenly very humble.

"Um… I'll have a gimlet," I say. Why the hell not? I

might hate it, but tonight is all about new things.

"A gimlet? God, the last person who ordered one of those must have been about seventy. And you look closer to seventeen, so let's see some ID."

"I'm old school," I say, handing over my fake ID.

The barmaid scrutinises it for a second, hands it back and asks, "Vodka or gin?"

"Just a gimlet, thanks."

"Yeah, but do you want a vodka gimlet or a gin gimlet?"

"Um, gin."

"When I was your age," says a voice to my right, "I couldn't handle anything stronger than cider."

I turn to see a man, probably in his late thirties or early forties, leaning against the bar. His hair is grey, but in that salt-and-pepper way that doesn't really look old, and he has a sharp, angular face.

"You don't know my age," I say, and my voice comes out all prim and proper. I know I don't look prim and proper tonight, and now the guy has a look on his face like he's accepting a challenge.

"Nineteen?"

"Right first time."

He grins and puts his hand up for a high five. I smack it, hard. My palm stings and tingles.

"Hey, can I ask you something?" I say.

"Sure, anything."

"What is it about nineteen?"

"What do you mean?"

"I get the impression that it's the sexiest age. For women, I mean. If someone's a stereotypical hot woman, like on a sitcom, she'll be a blonde nineteen-year-old. Or if a guy's describing a sexual fantasy, the woman seems to be nineteen, like, a disproportionate amount of the time."

The guy rests his chin on his hand and frowns. He seems to give this some serious consideration, before answering. "Youth is always attractive. Us blokes are programmed to be attracted to it because young women are more fertile. And even men who don't want kids, we've still got that caveman drive to reproduce, locked up in our DNA."

"But why nineteen specifically? A sixteen-year-old is young and fertile. A twenty-six-year-old is young and fertile."

"Sixteen's cutting it a bit fine. And twenty-six, I'll be honest with you love, is not the best age. Twenty-six-year-old girls have baggage like you wouldn't believe."

The barmaid hands me my gimlet. It looks like cloudy lemonade and the glass has a slice of lime on the rim. I take a sip and grimace. It's sharp as a diamond dagger.

"You'll get used to it," says the guy. I suddenly notice he's wearing a wedding ring. A plain gold band, simple and unmistakable. Strange. This conversation is anything but simple and unmistakable. I decide to end it before either of us does something stupid.

"Nice chatting to you," I say, and I take my horrible

drink and walk away from the bar without looking back.

I sit on my own for what feels like a very long time. I battle my way through the gimlet, then switch to a Snakebite. Not exactly classy, but I like the taste and the name. It's getting late, or at least starting to feel late, when I first see a woman watching me. She's sitting on her own a few tables away. Pretty, chubby, sunburnt, probably in her early thirties, and looking at me in a way I'm not used to being looked at by women. The novelty of it gives me a squirmy little thrill, and I smile at her. Her own smile, bright with pink lipstick, broadens. Then she gets up and walks clumsily over to me, banging her hip against a table and almost spilling her drink. Okay, she is clearly twice as drunk as me. Whatever this is, I have the upper hand.

"Made it," she says triumphantly as she sets her drink down on my table and pulls out a chair.

"Well done," I say, careful to sound friendly and encouraging rather than sarcastic.

She sits down, looks at me, and says, "Oh, shit."

"Nice to meet you too. Why oh shit?"

"Sorry, it's just... Honestly I was checking you out, and from a distance you look about twenty-five but up close you look about fifteen, so now I'm feeling like a perv."

"I'm seventeen. Don't tell the barmaid."

"God, you're just a kitten. And probably not into girls either."

"No, I don't think so."

"I'm an idiot. I'm Josie, by the way. And I'm sorry to

bother you. I swear I'm not usually like this; I don't just go up to girls in pubs and start chatting them up, not even in gay bars. I drank too much, and I never usually have more than a couple these days, but I've had a rough week so I felt like I deserved it. Actually, no, I didn't feel like I deserved it, but I felt like I needed it, you know what I mean?"

She talks really quickly – her words flowing into each other smoothly, like she's trying to sell me an expensive phone. Other than the way she talks, though, there's nothing smooth about her.

"Don't feel bad," I say. "I'm so bored I feel like peeling my own skin off. Stay and chat for a bit?"

She stays. And she doesn't just chat a bit, she *talks*. She tells me about her recent shitshow of a break-up.

"...and then he started threatening to kill himself. He said I'd thrown away a part of him so clearly he was disposable too. I mean, what do you say to that? Fucking brutal, right? I'm going back to women for sure. Don't get me wrong, they can be just as cruel but at least they're less melodramatic."

She tells me about the abortion that started the shitshow of a break-up.

"The girl sat next to me in the waiting room was about your age and she was reading a pamphlet on domestic violence and had bruises on her arm. And I felt ridiculous, like here are all these girls in terrible situations, and I'm a grown woman who just doesn't want what she's supposed to want. People keep telling me I'll change my mind about babies and it'll be too late. But they've been telling me I'll change my mind about babies since I was fifteen."

She even explains the sunburn.

"So when it was all over I went to the park, left my phone at home 'cause he was still messaging me a lot. I just wanted to escape, you know, I'm always wanting to escape, wherever I am. But I got to the park and spread out in the sunshine and actually wanted to stay there forever. It was the relief, I think, of not being pregnant and knowing my ex was on his way out of my life, even if he wasn't quite out of it yet. I just felt so fucking good, for the first time in months. But then I got a sunburn, so there you go. I can't stay anywhere for too long or I suffer for it."

While I'm listening, I kind of want to cry. Not because I feel bad for her, I'm just overwhelmed. And weirdly grateful. This woman is baring her soul to me and I didn't have to do anything. I didn't have to pry or spy or manipulate her in any way. She's just giving me everything, and it feels like a gift. A strange, inappropriate gift, like the kind your batty old great aunt might get you for Christmas, but still a gift.

Finally, she says "I've been going on about myself all night, I'm sorry. Let's talk about you for a change – what's your story?"

I consider this for a moment. Do I have a story? I think of primary school Literacy lessons – a story must have a beginning, a middle, and an end. If I do have a story, where the hell does it start? When does the middle part become the satisfying conclusion? I'm tempted to make a joke, but I feel like I owe this woman honesty.

"If I have a story, I don't think I'd be able to tell it very well. Not yet, at least."

"Fair enough. How about you just tell me what brings you to a scuzzy pub like this all on your own?"

"I did have a vague intention of losing my virginity tonight."

"Oh honey, and I've been wasting your time and bringing you down with my depressing stories."

"No, it's okay. I didn't actually *want* to lose my virginity. I just thought, if somebody wants to... you know. I'd let them."

Josie frowns. Her face is a fuzzy mixture of confused and concerned. "Look, it's none of my business, but are you sure this is the way you want to pop your cherry? Waiting in a pub for some random to come and pick you up? I mean, you don't seem all that enthusiastic. Maybe you're the type of girl who'd be better off waiting for someone she really likes."

It's late. She's drunk. I can tell her the truth. "I'm the type of girl who doesn't like anyone."

"What, sexually?"

"Sexually, romantically, all that stuff."

"So you've never even had a crush?"

I pause for a moment, skimming through my memories. "I had a crush on Spiderman when I was ten. I mean, I think it was a crush, but I don't remember wanting to kiss him or anything. And when I was fourteen there was this guy at school who sat next to me in English. My friend Angie said he fancied me and I got all psyched about it so I thought I must fancy him, too. But a couple of weeks later he asked me out and I said no, so I figured I must've got over him."

Josie takes the last, half-melted ice cube out of her glass and crunches it, looking pensive. "Have you ever thought you might be asexual?"

The word conjures up half-remembered science lessons. Bacteria reproducing by splitting in half. Stick insects having babies that are little clones of their mums. Algae and aphids.

"I can't reproduce on my own, as far as I know."

"No, I mean asexual like you don't experience sexual attraction."

"That's a thing?"

"Sure, my best mate's asexual. She's a little different though. She gets romantically attracted to men, like she's had boyfriends and fallen in love and everything. Just personally doesn't have any interest in sex."

"So there's like different flavours of asexual? It sounds complicated."

"Welcome to adult life, kitten. Nothing's simple."

We talk a little longer. I have a hundred questions, but I need to catch the last bus. Josie offers to walk me to the bus station, and I'm worried she might topple over and bust her ankle on the way to catch her own bus, so I say yes and we walk along arm in arm, like old friends.

"You take care," she says to me as we're hugging goodbye.

"You too," I say. And on a whim, I kiss her. I'm aiming for her cheek but I'm drunk and clumsy and the kiss lands on the corner of her mouth. She laughs a soft, snuffly laugh and kisses me back, on the corner of my mouth. Then she holds my head between her hands and says, "Everything works out in the end. Try not to worry too much, yeah?"

On the bus, my head spins from alcohol and confusion. I'm dizzy, and the long walk from the bus stop to home, lit by stars and the inadequate torch app on my phone, is difficult. I look up at the stars and for some reason I'm very aware that each one is a sun, with potential planets circling it, with potential lives being lived on them. I feel overwhelmed, but not in a bad way. Finally, I make it home and manage to sneak inside without making much noise. Upstairs, Darren's bedroom light is still on. I try to walk past softly, but inevitably he hears me and pokes his head round the door.

"Good night?" he whispers, looking like the cat who ate the canary. He likes seeing me all drunk and sloppy, it amuses him.

"Yes, actually," I say, standing up very straight and trying not to sway. "I feel like I made a real connection with someone."

"I can see that," he says, tapping the corner of his

mouth. Oh shit, Josie's pink lipstick. As I'm wiping it away, Darren starts singing Katy Perry's *I Kissed a Girl,* quietly and gleefully. Then he straightens his face out and says, "Seriously, though, you know it doesn't matter to me, right? Who you kiss, who you like, all of that. That kind of thing doesn't matter to anyone with half a brain."

His sincerity gives me a little boost of confidence. "I don't like anyone like that; I'm asexual," I say, trying the word on for size. Darren looks confused.

"Asexual, what does that mean?"

"I'm not sure. I have to Google it."

escape

chapter eighteen

Lana ran her fingertips cautiously over her left cheekbone. This hurt both her face, which was bruised and tender, and her fingers, which she'd hurt trying to defend herself. It was difficult to properly assess the damage without a mirror, but she had a black eye for sure. Possibly two. She really had to stop making people mad.

The guard had beaten her, not like a guard, but like a kid beating up another kid. All clumsy, frustrated rage. He didn't have kid-sized fists though. Lana sat in the tight space between the narrow bed and the wall of the cell with her knees brought up to her chin and tried to think about something else.

Movies. The Wizard of Oz. Though she would never admit it to anyone, she had damn-near cried when Judy Garland sang Over the Rainbow. There was something *about it; that young girl with her flat, grey life, longing for something different. It made Lana think of her own childhood. Those dresses made out of potato sacks that she had to wear when there weren't two nickels to rub together. And now, here she was in a grey prisoner's smock that looked a hell of a lot worse than those potato sack dresses.*

Footsteps sounded outside the door of the cell, then the door was noisily unlocked and opened. Lana tensed, expecting to see the guard who had beaten her, but fortunately it was a different one. This one was young and short and has a strangely wholesome look about him.

"I have to take you to see Doctor Richter," he said, trying to sound authoritative.

"What's your name?" said Lana, without moving.

"It's Jens Schreiber."

"It's nice to meet you, Jens. Could you please help me up? I'm a little sore."

Jens put out his hands and helped Lana to her feet, avoiding her eyes and looking at her bruised arms instead. With her body complaining every step of the way, Lana was led along the familiar corridors to Richter's laboratory.

It looked the same every time. Even the laboratory's occupants kept the same positions; Richter behind his desk, Scholz leaning up against the wall with his clipboard. Lana had long since figured out that Scholz was no scientist at all. He was simply a tough guy in a white coat, there in case she gave Richter any trouble.

Lana hated Richter. She hated his manners. She hated

his damn polygraph machine. She hated his habit of straying off topic, like last time when he had been questioning her about her activities in Paris last winter, and had gone off on a tangent about who she had lived with at the time, and what exactly the sleeping arrangements were. She hated the fact that she had to keep him off-topic as much as possible in order to avoid giving away crucial information, which meant giving him a lot of irrelevant details about her life.

She recoiled from his touch as he attached her to the polygraph. Every inch of her skin was sore, and his fleshy hands were unpleasantly warm.

"You might think I've not interviewed many women," he said, as he shuffled back around the desk and took his seat. "And you would be right. The vast majority of spies I interview are men. Certainly all the difficult cases I've worked with were men."

"I'm a difficult case? You flatter me."

"Your history is complicated to say the least, and you are evasive even after persuasive treatment."

Lana frowned – realizing that the phrase "persuasive treatment" referred to the beating she had been given – but only for a moment because frowning made her face hurt.

"Who exactly are you protecting?" Richter continued, leaning forward and folding his hands neatly on the desk. "And is he really worthy of your love and loyalty?"

Suddenly, Lana found herself suppressing the urge to smile. Richter might understand a great deal about her, but he also misunderstood a great deal. At last she had the upper hand.

That evening, Jens returned to her cell with the familiar, unappetizing and possibly poisoned bowl of stew. Lana was sitting on the bed, and watched him as he set it down carefully on the floor. Just as he was about to leave, Lana swung her legs down from the bed and stood up.

"Jens, will you stay a little while and talk?" she said, her voice quivering.

"What about?" said Jens warily.

"Oh, anything. The weather. The state of the roads. It's just," she took a step towards him, "I've been so damned lonely. And honestly, you remind me of a man I used to know."

A look of cautious understanding crossed the young guard's face, and he closed the door of the cell. Lana took another step towards him while he was facing the door, and when he turned back towards her she rested a hand lightly on his arm, then removed it swiftly.

"I don't know what I'm doing," she said, in a voice that was barely more than a whisper.

"It's all right," said Jens, whose chest was rising and falling rapidly. "You've been through a lot; it's understandable if you're feeling... mixed-up."

Their faces were inches apart now. Lana tilted her chin up, parted her lips and waited to be kissed. She did not have to wait long.

Jens slipped his arms around her waist, drawing her

towards him. Lana pressed her palms flat against his chest, dragging them down and slipping them up inside his jacket until she found what she wanted.

The gun was a Walther PPK. Not that Lana noticed this, in her hurry to bring it up to Jens' head and press the muzzle against his temple. He froze, and Lana pulled back to look at his face, which had turned the colour of sour milk.

"Don't scream, move, or do anything else," Lana whispered. "If you need to empty your bladder, that's fine, but don't make a fuss about it. I'm going to get out of here now, and I will do exactly what I need to do to get out of here. Hopefully that doesn't include shooting you, because you're very young and I'd like to give you a second chance."

nuts and bolts

I don't feel numb anymore. This is a mixed blessing, because I seem to be feeling everything at once. It's like everything that's happened over the past few months – everything from kissing Big Jimmy to the hens' untimely demise – is all coming at me, demanding my attention. Then there's the awkward process of figuring myself out regarding the whole "Am I asexual? Am I aromantic? What the hell is asexual? Is aromantic even a real word?" thing. It's weird, because I never thought I had to figure myself out before. I wanted to figure other people out, but as for myself… I guess I thought I could create myself, like a fictional character.

So I feel kind of overwhelmed and bruised and I keep crying at stupid things, like episodes of *Call the Midwife* and that Dogs Trust advert where all the dogs are looking for their "forever home." But I also feel alive, like an actual person. I decide to get a summer job, and Mum gets all over-enthusiastic when I tell her this and is straight on the phone to Scott Burchill, a friend of Dad's and one of the local farmers. I'm anticipating an interview. Quite looking forward to getting dressed up, doing my hair in a neat bun, and wearing a blazer. But of course that's not how things are done around here. When Mum gets off the phone, she says "He'll see you at nine on Monday. He says to wear clothes that you don't mind getting dirty."

At nine o'clock on Monday, it's already hot and the sun is dazzling. I stand at Scott's gate, watching him trudge up the dusty path in his familiar dark grey overalls. I've known Scott all my life and think of him as a non-biological uncle. He's sixty-ish, tall, and stubbly. Mum refers to him as a "confirmed bachelor" which I used to think meant that he doesn't like women. Then Dad explained that he likes women too much to marry just the one of them.

"All right, Hollywood?" he yells. This is presumably in reference to my red-rimmed, cat's eye sunglasses, which I bought on the first hot day of the year. They don't go with my outfit of old jeans and a faded, orange t-shirt, but I like them.

"All right, Scott?" I shout back, pushing my sunglasses up on top of my head.

"You dyed your hair!"

"Yeah. I'm getting bored of it though; I might try some other colour."

"Which one?"

"Oh, I don't know. Purple, maybe? Green?" I'm half-joking. Scott chuckles (He is the only person I know whose laugh can properly be called a chuckle) but also shakes his head in despair at "girls these days".

He unlocks the gate as a first day formality – I could easily climb over it. We head down the path together, with my trainers and his wellies kicking up swirls of dry, pale dirt-dust.

"Did your mum explain what the job is?"

"She said you need some help sorting and fixing equipment."

"Well, just sorting really. I've had a ton of nuts and bolts delivered and they need sorting by size and screwing together."

We're at the barn now. Red-walled, grey-roofed. Spacious enough for kids to play chase games inside – I remember that, though I don't remember who I was playing with. Scott unbolts the door.

"What else do you need help with? After I've sorted all the nuts and bolts."

"I'll let you know once you're finished," says Scott, as we step into the straw-scented darkness of the barn. He flicks on a light, and my jaw drops.

"So when you said a ton of nuts and bolts, you meant *literally* a ton?"

"Yep."

"What do you need a ton of nuts and bolts for?"

"I don't, but they were a steal. I'll sell 'em on once they're sorted."

"They weren't *literally* a steal, were they?"

Scott just laughs, and I stare in dismay at the enormous heap of metal in front of me. This is crazy. This is like one of those impossible tasks that men get given in fairy tales to prove they're worthy of marrying the princess. This is going to take all summer.

"Not the most interesting job, I'm afraid," says Scott. "But there's a radio to listen to and you won't be on your own. The other kid should be here in just under an hour."

There's nothing for it but to ignore the ridiculous hugeness of the task, grit my teeth, and dive in. I soon realise that there are only five different sizes of nuts and bolts, and whenever I manage to match a pair, it is a tiny victory. I put the sorted and matched pairs into large, empty buckets that Scott has left for the purpose and work steadily, listening to Radio One from a little black oblong of a radio that fuzzes if I get too close to it. My jeans acquire a layer of grime from sitting on the floor of the barn.

So, I have the world's most boring summer job. I'm not too bothered by this, though. The simple, repetitive actions kind of feel like a penance for all the stupid shit I've done over the past few months. Like what Catholics do with the rosary beads.

Sure enough, the other kid arrives in just under an hour. I'm so absorbed in the work that I don't notice until he and Scott are in the doorway of the barn, which is kept open to let the breeze in.

"Hollywood, this is Dumbledore. Dumbledore, this is Hollywood," says Scott. He nicknames everyone.

Well, this is a very awkward situation. It's mostly awkward because Dumbledore is Ethan – my former best friend who I then hugely offended by friend-zoning. It's also awkward because the character on Ethan's t-shirt is not actually Dumbledore, it's Gandalf. Gandalf is pointing at me, Lord Kitchener style, and the text beneath him reads, "I want YOU for an adventure."

"I'll leave you two to get on with it," says Scott, and he walks away so quickly and quietly that it seems tactful, like someone leaving the room so a would-be couple can be alone together. Should I say something funny? That's my first instinct, but I've no idea how much Ethan hates me right now. His face, as usual, is giving nothing away.

"I didn't have the heart to tell him," says Ethan.

"What?"

"That it's Gandalf, not Dumbledore." He gestures vaguely to his t-shirt.

I half-rise onto my knees and stick my hand out. "I'm Gwen. Nice to meet you."

Ethan smiles his rare, Mona Lisa smile and bends down to shake my hand. "I'm Ethan."

There. A fresh start, if such a thing is possible. A second chance. I'm still tense and uncomfortable, but at least there's an unspoken agreement that we will both try not to screw this up.

"So when Scott said he had a ton of nuts and bolts to sort, he meant *literally* a ton?"

"Yeah, I didn't realise either."

Ethan stares at the gigantic metallic pile which glints in the light from the bare bulb overhead and the sunshine flowing in from the open doors. "If you squint, it looks like dragon treasure."

I squint. It looks nothing like dragon treasure, but I like that he sees it that way.

friends

When your job is sorting an endless pile of nuts and bolts and you only have one colleague, you really don't have any choice but to talk to them. If you didn't, you'd probably go crazy. So me and Ethan talk. A little at first, about safe things like how hot it is or whatever song is on the radio. Then a lot, about everything. He asks me how I've been and it would be so easy to pretend. To be a different person, living a different life. But instead, I tell him more-or-less everything that's happened since I broke up with Martine and Angie. He doesn't say much, just listens.

Halfway through the second week of working together, we have sorted bucketfuls of nuts and bolts but the pile is still pretty big. Ethan, being chubby, is suffering in the heat and works slowly.

"You know my cousin Dawn?" he says, languidly screwing a nut and bolt together and tossing them into the appropriate bucket.

"Yeah."

"She's at uni now, and when I told her about this job she told me about a Nut and Screw party she went to during fresher's week."

"What's that?"

"All the girls get given a nut, and all the boys get given a bolt, and you're supposed to mingle and talk to each other and find the nut that matches your bolt, or the bolt that matches your nut."

"That sounds… Freudian." I can hear the distaste in my own voice. I probably sound like a prude but I don't care. I'm sure as hell not pretending that sounds like a great way to meet people.

"Apparently Dawn got given a really big nut, so every guy she spoke to… well, their bolts were too small, and they were all apologetic about it."

I giggle in spite of myself. I remember Dawn as tall and curvy and confident – probably intimidating when she wants to be.

"I thought people would've got over their obsession with sex by the time they get to uni."

"Really? All those people living away from their parents for the first time – I reckon they're more eager than ever."

"Great. So when exactly do people calm down? When does life stop revolving around sex?"

"Probably when you're married with kids and you're exhausted all the time."

I shake my head in dismay. There's a charged silence. Ethan is organising his thoughts, I can tell.

"So, I just wanted to say sorry," he says, not looking at me.

"What for?"

"For guilt-tripping you about mixed signals and friend-zoning and stuff. I think if I'd known your friend-zone was empty, I would've been less of a dick about it."

"Thank you. And I'm sorry for saying I didn't like you. Partly because it was mean but mostly because it was bullshit. I like you a lot, just not romantically."

"And I'm okay with that, honestly. I just got frustrated because it happens a lot. Girls liking me, just not in that way."

"Yeah, I guess that'd suck for most guys. But in my case at least, it's nothing to do with you."

"Oh, come on, you don't have to do the whole It's not you, it's me thing.'"

"But it is me. I'm just not interested in relationships." We can have the talk about labels (I'm increasingly sure that mine are "asexual" and "aromantic") later. I'm too hot and tired at the moment.

"Fair enough. I'm probably too interested in relationships. I'm trying to chill out about it though, and not fall for every girl who's vaguely nice to me. Apparently that's not healthy."

"So…" Here we go, the million pound question. "We're okay?"

"Yeah, we're good."

"Do you maybe want to hang out sometime? Do something other than screwing?"

He laughs explosively. "I would love that. All this screwing is giving me repetitive strain injury."

"And it's so boring."

"And it's too hot and sweaty."

So that's how Ethan and I became friends the second time around. On Friday, we collect our week's wages from Scott, then walk back to Ethan's house to hang out. The heat has finally broken, though it's still sunny. I have a pocketful of cash and all is right with the world. For the moment, at least.

The house is empty, with both of Ethan's parents still at work. I haven't been here in years, and the wallpaper in the hall is different, but the place still smells the same. A homey, toasty smell that makes me think of elevenses. When I was little, elevenses were never a thing at my house, so they were one of the advantages of hanging out at Ethan's.

"So what do you want to do?" says Ethan, shutting the front door behind him.

"I want to see your room. I mean, if that's okay." I'm not exactly sure why it wouldn't be okay, but I get the feeling I have to be careful, just for a little while.

I follow him upstairs and into his room, and I guess I was more nervous than I realised because I can feel the tension leaving my shoulders. Looking around, it becomes clear that Ethan is pretty much the same person I was friends with all those years ago. Taller and more weighed down with baggage, like all of us, but basically the same. He still has dragon posters, for example, though admittedly one of these posters features some kind of warrior woman in impractical metal underwear. He has just as many action figures as he did at eleven, and the stack of board games in the corner is definitely taller.

"Okay, how come you have more toys now than when you were eleven?"

"What, I should have less toys?"

"Most people do."

"But life is easy at eleven. It gets harder as you grow up, so surely it makes sense to have more toys. For escapism."

There's no arguing with that. I sit down on Ethan's bed, then stand up again, unsure of where to put myself. We're wasting time.

"Sorry for being awkward," I say. "Honestly, I haven't had any male friends in a very long time. It's been a long time since I hung out with friends and did anything other than watch romcoms."

"You like romcoms?"

"Yeah, I love them."

"But I thought you weren't into… romantic stuff."

"I'm not, but I always wanted to be one of the women in romantic comedies. Live somewhere exciting like New York and have some glamorous job at a magazine and a beautiful flat and perfect nails."

"Yeah, I get that. I don't have any romcoms to watch, I'm afraid."

"That's okay, I wouldn't put you through that."

"We could watch *The Terminator* and paint each other's nails, as a compromise."

I laugh, but that is exactly what we end up doing. We stretch out on Ethan's bed, watch Arnie kick arse, and paint each other's nails a rich plum colour. I decide not to ask why Ethan owns nail polish. My best guess is that it's something to do with LARPing, but I could be wrong. Maybe he has a girly side that I don't know about yet. A few weeks ago, I wouldn't have been satisfied, not knowing something about someone. But maybe I don't have to know everything about everyone, at least not right away.

When the movie finishes we go down to the kitchen for food, just as Ethan's mum, Moira, gets back from work. She's surprised to see me, and keeps looking from me to Ethan, then back to me, like she's trying to figure out the exact nature of the connection between us.

"So how have you been, hen?" That's not a nickname, she calls all women and girls "hen." She's very Scottish.

"Not bad, thanks. How about you?"

"Ah, you know. I keep telling myself I'll slow down with work and all my bloody projects but I never do. Ethan, what are you planning on feeding this girl? And don't say bacon sandwiches."

"Err, macaroni cheese?" Ethan looks at me questioningly.

"That's fine," says Moira, "as long as it's not the one out of a packet – that's for emergencies only."

I always thought there was just macaroni cheese from a packet and macaroni cheese from a tin, but it turns out there is a third kind. Ethan teaches me how to make a cheese sauce, boils up some pasta, and serves each of us a generous bowlful. I fork up a mouthful straight away and it's delicious. Ethan agrees but adds a pinch of chilli powder to his, completely missing the point of comfort food. Moira has disappeared upstairs so we commandeer the living room and eat in front of the TV. I could eat this macaroni cheese every day. It's addictive. Crackaroni cheese.

It also seems to have a mild sedative effect, because me and Ethan both get dozy watching *Tattoo Fixers*. We've got the lights off to see the TV better (we used to watch movies like this when we were kids and pretend we were at the cinema) and it seems later than it is. I slump against Ethan and tell him I'd like to get a tattoo of a dragonfly. He tells me he wants a tattoo of a dragon. I'm not sure which of us falls asleep first.

When I wake up, my head is in the crook of Ethan's

shoulder. I can hear him breathing steadily, and after a moment I realise that we are breathing perfectly in sync. This is going to sound weird, but I feel like we are a pair of lungs, separate and connected at the same time. And this is something I like. Something I want. Maybe with just one other person, or maybe with a few people, or maybe with everyone in the world.

fox

Time is weird. It's especially weird during the summer holidays. When the weather's hot and there's not much going on, it seems to move extra slowly. Half an hour spent on the sofa, spooning with a bag of frozen peas as the temperature skyrockets, feels like a whole day. Ten minutes on the bus into town, arguing about who is the greatest movie villain (Ethan thinks it's either Jack Nicholson in *The Departed* or Jack Nicholson as The Joker. I think it's every Disney villainess ever) feels like a small eternity. But as soon as the sun goes down, it seems like the day disappeared all too quickly.

School starts tomorrow. I am beyond anxious. No matter how many times I tell myself that this is a fresh start, I can't convince myself. There are no fresh starts. No second chances. Being inside the house gives me a cooped-up, restless feeling, so I go out into the garden. I stand at the bottom of the garden, in front of our less-than-picturesque fence made of half-rotted fence posts and two strings of barbed wire. I look out over the fields and stare at the sunset, hoping this will calm me down. It doesn't. The sky looks apocalyptic and the sun is a glob of molten metal, sinking towards the horizon where it will surely pour itself all over the fields, burning everything.

In the distance, I see a sudden flash of copper, half-hidden in a patch of long grass. A fox. My mind goes blank instantly and all I can do is watch it, tracking its movements, all my muscles tensed and senses slightly heightened. It's strange how wild animals can do that – take you out of your mind and into your body.

As the fox gets closer, I can see that it's not just any fox. It's *the* fox. The one with the dark belly. The hen killer. A vision of blood and feathers and dead, uneaten birds creeps out of the dusty corner of my brain that I shoved it into. I back away from the fence, keeping my eyes on the fox, and I'm edging towards the shed, unsure of what I'm doing.

The fox is halfway across the field when I reach the door of the shed. I am done moving slowly. I whip inside and grab the air rifle, loading it swiftly, and as I leave the shed I slip out of my wellies because I want this to be quick and quiet. The fox is nosing the grass, probably smelling something interesting. I must be upwind, or it would have smelled me. Coffee on my breath. The lingering scent of Snow Fairy shower gel on my skin. Sweat. It would have smelled the messy, conflicting odors of human and run. When I get to the fence, I put the air rifle on the ground and pull apart the two strings of barbed wire, making the gap wide enough to step through. Then I pick up the gun and take a few strides towards the fox.

I swing the air rifle up into position. At the exact same moment, the fox brings its head up from the grass and looks at me. Its coat glows blood-red in the evening light. I could kill this animal and not feel guilty at all. Finger on the trigger. A nice, clear shot.

"BANG!" I shout, and the fox snaps into motion, scarpering away across the field.

There you go, hen killer – a second chance. Don't waste it.

discoveries

chapter twenty

On the bus to school, my stomach is a nest of snakes. I feel like I'm going to vomit, and have to keep telling myself "Gwen, you will not throw up. You have a very weak gag reflex which, as an asexual woman, is not as useful as it could be, but it is a blessing today."

About halfway through the morning I start to calm down, because things aren't half as bad as they could be. I'm not naïve enough to think that people have forgotten the Mimi business, but the summer has given them other things to think about. No doubt there have been exotic travels and holiday romances and family dramas that all need discussing. There's still a part of me itching to find out all the gossip, but I manage to ignore it. A couple of people give me the stink eye, but nothing more dramatic than that happens. I'm just thinking that I can deal with this, that this year needn't be a total disaster if I just keep my head down and concentrate on my A levels, when two unexpected things happen.

The first is the appearance of Mr. Ackerly. As I walk from Geography to Spanish, I see him marching down the corridor with a bunch of papers under his arm. He nods at me as he passes, not smiling. The sight of him is jarring, and I realise that I expected him to be gone for good after Mimi set the rumour mill into motion. I don't know how I feel about this. How I am supposed to feel depends, of course, on whether he actually did anything wrong. But there's no way of knowing whether he's a predatory creep or a helpless victim of the worst kind of gossip.

The second unexpected thing happens at lunchtime. I go to the toilets, and when I'm done peeing I hear sniffling, snuffling sounds coming from the cubicle next to mine. It sounds like someone trying to get their crying under control, and not being very successful. There is a tiny, broken-sounding sob.

I tap softly on the cubicle wall. This is super-inappropriate, especially considering I've been trying to get better at respecting boundaries, but whatever.

"Are you okay?" There's no reply, just some more muffled crying. "You can tell me to piss off if you want, but maybe telling someone what's up would help?"

Silence. Then, in a thick, familiar voice, "After everything I did, he's still fucking *here*."

My brain explodes. The first reason for this explosion

is the realisation that the girl crying in the cubicle next to me is Martine. Her voice is unmistakable, even though it's hoarse from crying. It feels like a lifetime since I last spoke to her. The second, more significant reason for this brain explosion is the realisation that Martine is Mimi. Shy, bookwormy Martine. Martine the nervous giggler. Martine who is afraid of spiders but won't let anybody kill them because it's cruel. She's the one who turned the school upside down.

"Martine?"

"Yeah?"

"It's Gwen."

"I know."

"…"

"…"

"Do you want to go to the library?"

"Yes, please."

Martine finds it comforting to be surrounded by books. She once told me that the smell of them is soothing, which I didn't understand because books don't smell like anything special to me. Just paper and glue. But then she told me that being surrounded by books is like being surrounded by hundreds of different worlds. Hundreds of different places to escape to. And I understood that.

In the library, we go up the stairs and retreat to the furthest, most dimly-lit corner. We sit on the floor, between a wall of books and an actual wall, tucked away and invisible. Martine isn't crying anymore but her eyes are bloodshot and she doesn't seem eager to talk, so I look at the books, giving her a moment to just breathe and get her shit together.

There are a lot of historical novels on these shelves. Curly fonts on the spines. Big dresses on the front covers. The kind of thing Martine likes to read. I spot a trilogy of books that I remember her reading and re-reading – for about a year, she always had one of them in her bag. *The Governess Trilogy*, I think it's called. I pick one of the three off the shelf and start reading the blurb. *Miryam Hardcastle – Mimi to her intimate acquaintances – is not the timid yet hardworking governess she appears to be.* Huh. So that's where she got the name Mimi from.

"So is this Mimi an interesting character?" I ask, fake-casual, waving the book at Martine.

"Seriously?" she says, giving me a slightly sour look. "I tried to persuade you to read *The Governess Trilogy* for months."

I shrug, and carry on reading the blurb. "It says here she uncovers a big scandal, but then she gets embroiled in a scandal of her own. There were a lot of scandals in the olden days, weren't there?"

"I guess."

"What does embroiled mean?"

"Involved. Involved in something bad."

"Oh. I thought it was something to do with cooking."

"You're thinking of *broiled*."

I put the book back on the shelf, then say, "I think you

should tell me about it."

"The book?"

"No, not the book. You know what. At least tell me the part that involves my phone."

Martine looks like she's going to cry again, but she doesn't. "I don't know where to start."

"The beginning? For the sake of tradition."

martine's story

Martine was supposed to be meeting Angie in Starbucks. It was a hot day, so they would buy those strange hybrid drinks that were half-tea and half-lemonade and tasted like fruit squash that had been diluted so much you couldn't tell what fruit it was supposed to be. Then they would go shopping. But Angie was late, again. Martine looked at the message on her phone, which read, "Sorry, I got held up. Blame Sam. ;)" She did not blame Sam, because Sam was a teenage boy, and Martine had been brought up to believe that teenage boys were slaves to their hormones. This was why she usually avoided them.

She ought to be happy for Angie. She and Sam were a cute couple, and Martine couldn't argue with cute. Still, there was no denying that she was seeing less and less of Angie, and with Gwen out of the picture, she was really feeling the loss.

Sunshine poured through the windows of the Starbucks and did battle with the inefficient air conditioning. Martine took her tall iced green tea lemonade and pressed the cup against her cheek, then her neck, letting the condensation cool her overheated skin. She was just about to start reading *The Great Gatsby* when Mr. Ackerly walked through the door.

He didn't notice her at first, so she watched him while he stood in the queue, looking at all the cakes and sandwiches behind the counter. Martine thought he looked hungry, but he didn't buy a snack. She sucked up her tall iced green tea lemonade through a straw and felt her stomach fill with butterflies. It was odd, seeing him outside of school, but not as odd as it could have been. If it had been Mrs. Morton, her English Lit. teacher, ordering a cappuccino, that would have been thoroughly weird. Martine got on well enough with teachers because she was quiet and she did her homework, but she still found it difficult to think of them as actual people, with lives outside of school. Mr. Ackerly was different, though. The barista handed him his coffee and then he was turning, looking for a place to sit, and the butterflies inside Martine went berserk because he was going to see her.

By the time he spotted her, Martine was already smiling. She had a striking smile – large, very white teeth in a dark face – and she used it to soften people up, whether they needed softening or not. She liked other people to be as soft as possible, because this was how she saw herself. Soft all the way through, except for her bright, smiling teeth. Mr. Ackerly smiled back, walking towards her, and she tried (for the third time) to find the word that matched his smile. She had already tried and discarded charming, crooked, rakish, roguish and boyish. Wolfish, that was it. "Hi, Mr. Ackerly."

"Hi, Martine. Keeping cool?"

"Mostly."

"Is it okay if I sit here? There don't seem to be any other seats."

"Of course."

"I promise I'll disappear as soon as your friends get here. Wouldn't want to embarrass you."

Martine didn't know what to say to that. Part of her would have loved nothing more than for Angie to arrive at that exact moment and see her having a drink with an actual adult man. Part of her hoped that Angie would message her again, saying she was sorry but she couldn't make it today.

"Um, sorry to be direct about this," said Mr. Ackerly, and Martine's heartbeat sped up in anticipation of this directness. "But I think you have ink on your face."

Oh god. The barista had written her name on the cup. Now there was nothing but a faint, bluish smudge. Her first instinct was to make a dash for the toilets, but she had wet wipes in her bag and Mr. Ackerly kept reassuring her that it wasn't that obvious. So she wet wiped her face and her neck, and asked four times if the ink was all gone. Each time, some of the stubborn stuff remained, hiding in the crevices of her face. Eventually, Mr. Ackerly said, "Here, let me," and took the wet wipe from her. He dabbed at her face, just beside her nose, and Martine could feel the warmth of his fingers through the thin, cool cloth. At this point, her embarrassment was finally eclipsed. To be cleaned like this felt both familiar and very, very new.

The fear that Martine felt around people she didn't know well – mild and manageable, but always there – disappeared, and she found she could talk easily to Mr. Ackerly. They talked about books, especially *The Great Gatsby* (one of his recommendations) and she even found the guts to ask him the things she'd been wondering, ever since she took him the papier-mâché donkey's head for *A Midsummer Night's Dream*. His first name was Drew, short for Andrew. He was twenty-eight. He had a pet cat named Oscar.

By the time he finished his coffee, Martine felt like she knew him and it seemed only natural for them to arrange to have coffee again. Not that Martine had been drinking coffee, but the word coffee was a tricky one. Coffee rarely meant just coffee. He left, and when Angie arrived three minutes later, she found Martine starry-eyed and maybe a tiny bit in love.

They met for coffee three times and talked about everything under the sun. Drew gave Martine the rare thrill of being looked at and listened to simultaneously –

usually it was one or the other. The third time, they were talking about movies when Martine admitted she'd never seen *Annie Hall*. This, apparently, was a gaping wound in her consciousness that had to be bandaged immediately.

And that was how Martine ended up in Drew's flat, watching *Annie Hall* from a soft leather sofa. As she watched, she became gradually more and more aware that she was being watched. Oscar the cat – a slightly overweight tabby – sat on the arm of the sofa and stared brazenly at her. Drew sat on the other side of her, and watched her more subtly. Gauging her reactions to the film, perhaps.

His glances at Martine were swift at first, then lingering. Then his hand was on her thigh, about halfway between her knee and... about halfway up. She could feel the warmth of it through her jeans.

It wasn't right. If they had already kissed, perhaps it would be different, but Martine had a sequence of events that had to unfold in the right order, or she felt off-balance and a little dirty. If she kissed him – lightly and sweetly – that would take them back to the top of the sequence and she would feel better. She leaned towards him, lips slightly parted. He lunged forward, kissed her firmly, and put his hand right between her legs.

The shock of it sent a jolt of adrenaline rushing through her and she pushed him away, hard. He looked stunned, and Martine giggled nervously, waiting for the apology. Something about getting carried away. An earnest plea for forgiveness, or maybe panic because Martine was a student. Not his student, and well over sixteen, but still…

There was no apology. No excuses. No visible fear. Drew straightened himself up, and his face gave nothing away. Martine managed to stop giggling, but she still smiled because she was afraid now and needed to defuse the situation. Drew leaned towards her again, and there was something determined in the set of his jaw. Martine jumped up from the sofa. "I better go," she said, and walked straight out of Drew's living room and down the hall to the front door without looking back.

When she got to the door, she couldn't open it – it was stuck. She could hear Drew's footsteps coming down the hall and a hundred gothic heroines swirled around her brain in their ethereal white nightgowns, calling her a stupid bitch, telling her she had walked right into a trap.

"I think you got the wrong idea," said Drew from right behind her. His voice made Martine flinch but his tone, at least, was reasonable. "You shouldn't have kissed me. I know we've been getting along well but I only meant to be friendly. Anything more would be inappropriate."

Martine's fingers slipped from the doorknob and she turned to face him. She was shaking, but not entirely with fear. "I shouldn't have kissed you? What about what *you* did?"

"And what exactly did I do?"

Through the fog of adrenaline settling over her brain,

Martine searched desperately for the words to describe what he had done. But she couldn't find them. She didn't even know what to call the part of her body he had touched. Romance novels had nothing but stupid euphemisms and biology textbooks had only taught her about the inside parts. Now Mr. Ackerly – he was no longer Drew – was smiling, just a tiny bit at one corner of his mouth. It was a look of triumph, because he knew for certain that Martine would never tell.

"Do you want me to open the door for you?" he asked, and Martine wanted to slap his face and punch his stomach and call him a pervert, a bastard, an unprincipled scoundrel, a cunt. But as much as she wanted all that, what she wanted more was to get away. She nodded sharply.

"What's the magic word?"

Martine clenched her jaw and said, "Please." It was the most disgusting word she had ever said.

She took the bus home, sweating in the heat, then had a long shower. She washed herself thoroughly all over, except for the place where Mr. Ackerly had touched her. She didn't even want her own hands there, so she just washed her stomach and let the soapy water run downwards.

There was no question of telling her parents. Even if she had been able to gather her thoughts and shape them into coherent sentences, how could she explain that she had gone to a teacher's house and willingly kissed him? She still remembered the telling-off Mama had given her for buying a bikini.

Telling Angie was another impossibility. Angie was distracted these days, forgetting to reply to messages and only half-listening to Martine when they talked, unless they were talking about Sam. There was a good chance that Martine would tell Angie what had happened – haltingly, painfully – only for her to look blank and say, "Sorry, I spaced out for a minute. What were you saying?" There was also a chance that Angie's protective instincts would go into overdrive and she would do something stupid. March right into the staff room at school, possibly dragging Martine by the wrist, and loudly announce what had happened. Or, even worse, go to Mr. Ackerly's flat and confront him. Whichever way Martine looked at it, telling Angie was too much of a risk.

The only other person Martine could imagine talking to was Gwen. But she'd blocked her on social media and even deleted Gwen's number from her phone after the incident with Big Jimmy. The idea of walking up to a girl who probably hated her and casually trying to start a conversation, with the weight of everything that had happened pressing down on her, was absurd.

The first day of school after the incident was a bad day. Not that Martine saw Mr. Ackerly, but she was constantly afraid that she would. She found herself checking the corridors before leaving a classroom, scanning crowds in search of his face. Although she didn't want him to see her, she found that she wanted to see him.

She wanted to keep an eye on him, to make sure no other girls found themselves alone with him. Knowing what she knew, and feeling so utterly helpless about it, was sickening.

It rained heavily for most of the day, and people crowded inside during lunch time, giving the school a claustrophobic feel. Wet shoes left streaks of dirty water on corridor floors and everything smelled damp. Martine didn't have any appetite for lunch, so she went to the library instead of the canteen and checked out a couple of books. Then she went to the Sixth Form common room, planning to get stuck into *The Other Boleyn Girl.* Hopefully that would take her mind off things for a while.

Just beyond the door to the common room was a row of coats on pegs. On one of these pegs was a coat that Martine recognised as Gwen's. A charcoal-coloured trench coat type thing. Cheap, but nicely cut. It made Gwen look a bit like an old-fashioned lady detective. Martine peeked around the corner and saw Gwen sitting at one of the little round tables. For once, she wasn't on her phone. She seemed to be doing homework, probably in a last-minute rush. There was no way Martine could just go up to Gwen and talk to her, now or at any other time. But another possibility presented itself.

She reached out a tentative hand and felt the pockets of Gwen's coat. One of them contained a phone-shaped heaviness. If she could just find Gwen's number, she would be able to send her a message. Maybe they would be able to patch things up and then, just possibly, Gwen could help her figure out what to do about Mr. Ackerly.

Checking to make sure no-one was about to enter the common room, Martine fished Gwen's phone out of her coat pocket and prayed that she hadn't changed her password. She hadn't. However, the moment Martine had access to the contents of Gwen's phone, her plan was de-railed.

There were folders labelled "sad stuff", "sex stuff", "love stuff" and "miscellaneous". She momentarily forgot about getting Gwen's number and opened up "love stuff". The contents made her head spin. Perhaps it was the shock of opening this Aladdin's cave of gossip that made her forget her sense of right and wrong. She had never stolen anything before, but she didn't deliberate or hesitate before slipping the phone into the pocket of her own coat.

Locked in a toilet cubicle, Martine combed through the contents of the phone and marvelled at them. How the hell had Gwen found out all this stuff? And why? And why did Martine feel all tingly and hyped-up? It occurred to her that for the first time in days, she did not feel completely helpless. She had a weapon now, and a plan began to form around it.

There was no need to tell any teachers what had happened with Mr. Ackerly. There was probably no need to tell anyone. Instead, she was going to get everyone's attention (anonymously, of course – she wanted people listening to her, not looking at her) and then she was going to create a scandal. She had read enough Jane Austen to know that a scandal could ruin someone, and she fully intended to ruin Mr. Ackerly.

bite the bullet

chapter twenty-one

I always assumed Mimi was somebody tech-savvy enough to get past the password protection on my phone. Martine is not remotely tech-savvy, but she has known my password for months.

It is last November, and me and Martine and Angie are all getting drunk on cherry schnapps at Angie's house. We were supposed to be going out, but we drank too much while we were doing our hair and make-up, then got sloppy and started giving each other stupid hairstyles. None of us are very good at drinking.

"There. You look like a sexy pineapple," says Angie, patting the spiky ridiculousness of my new hairdo. I look in Angie's bedroom mirror and laugh, and can't stop laughing. Angie kneels behind me with her arms around my waist and she laughs as well, our shoulders shaking in unison.

"Angieeeeee, why don't you have any good books?" Martine's voice is muffled because she is lying on the floor with a large hardback book about some rugby player open across her face.

"That *is* a good book," Angie insists.

"It's non-fiction," says Martine, pulling the book down off her face and resting it on her chest. "I like *stories*. Stories are the best. And words, I love words."

"You can't love all the words," says Angie. "What about moist?"

"Ew."

"Moist, moist, moist, MOIST!"

"Ugh, stop it."

"What's your favourite word?" I say, trying to change the subject before a fight breaks out.

"Serendipity," says Martine, with certainty.

"Yeah, that's a good one," I agree. "Kind of musical."

"Serendippytit," says Angie, looking thoughtful. "What does it mean?"

Me and Martine both burst out laughing, and then the three of us try to decide on the meaning of the word "serendippytit." We come to the obvious conclusion that it means lucky boobs.

"This is my new favourite word," I announce, digging my phone out of my handbag. "I'm changing my password to serendippytit."

At some point, while Martine was telling me what happened with Mr. Ackerly and my phone and everything, I took hold of her hand. Now she's done with the telling, I'm still holding it. Her palm is all sweaty. Or maybe mine is, I'm not sure.

"I'm really sorry," she says. "For taking your phone, and for what I did with it."

"Would you still be sorry if it'd worked? If Mr. Ackerly had been fired."

"Yes. Though… I'd be a lot less sorry."

"You know, you're kind of a ruthless bitch," I say, and it comes out sounding weirdly affectionate.

"I know. Though I didn't know that about myself until recently."

"I didn't know that about you until just now. Um… this is gonna sound soppy, but I'd really like to get to know you again."

"That'd be nice."

Martine gives my hand a little squeeze, then lets go and stands up.

"Where are you going?"

"To get this over with before I lose my nerve. Will you come with me?"

We stand in front of the staff room door, side by side. Martine is wide-eyed and shaking.

"My heart's pounding," she whispers.

I should say something comforting, but I'm afraid for her. Afraid of what's going to happen. Afraid of how brave some people have to be.

"Mine too," I admit. Martine raises a fist and knocks on the door.

a little while later

chapter twenty-two

Mr. Ackerly has been fired. Quietly. Well, it was obviously intended to be a quiet and discreet disappearance, but as soon as he stopped showing up to classes, the rumors and gossip filled the air like midges on a summer evening. Although Martine says she just wants to forget about it, I know a part of her is happy about this. He has a reputation now. A stain, or a stink, attached to his name.

Martine offers to tell people (and by people she means, like, everyone) that she was behind the whole Mimi thing, but I tell her not to bother because seriously, who needs more drama? The real reason I tell her not to bother is that I feel like she deserves a break.

I do ask her to explain things to Angie, though. Angie apparently does a lot of talking and crying and hugging with Martine, and then she seeks me out in the canteen on a Monday lunchtime and we do a lot of talking and crying and hugging. Angie swears never to tell about Martine being Mimi, and she also swears to protect me from anyone who acts like a dick because they still think I'm Mimi. Angie's protection is not to be sneezed at – she's a Rottweiler when she wants to be.

The three of us have a lot to catch up on, so we decide to hang out at Martine's house after school. Martine's in a good mood, and as we hang our coats on the backs of chairs in her kitchen, she announces that she's going to bake a cake.

"No offence, but is it going to be one of those sugar-free, fat-free, gluten-free things?" I ask tentatively.

"No, I'm done with clean eating. I missed chocolate too much. And Mama got all upset when I wouldn't eat her Gato Patate."

Me and Angie get ready to pitch in, but Martine handles most of the cake-making herself. It's a super-simple cake, just sugar, butter, eggs, and flour. Martine bungs it in the oven, and the three of us sit at the kitchen table with mugs of tea and wait for it to be ready, while a delicious cake-y scent fills the air.

"Hey, um… I know I never really apologised for the thing with Big Jimmy," I begin awkwardly, knowing this is a risky topic to bring up, but wanting to get it out of the way so I can enjoy my cake.

"Actually, you never apologised at all," Angie pipes up, but she looks more amused than offended.

"Yeah, well, I'm sorry. I know it's way too late, but I'm sorry for kissing him. I think there's certain rules that I'm never really going to understand, but that doesn't make it okay to just ignore them."

"Aw, honey, don't be sorry," says Martine. "We totally overreacted."

"Yeah, sorry for saying stupid crap," adds Angie.

"Anyway, I don't even like Big Jimmy any more, I haven't liked him for months."

I chew this over. "So you're done liking Big Jimmy, and you're done with the diet."

"It's not a diet, it's a lifestyle. Remember?" Angie nudges Martine teasingly and Martine cringes, as if the person she was six months ago is an embarassing younger sister.

"So, what's new with you, Angie? Apart from Sam."

"I got my bellybutton pierced."

"You're kidding."

Angie whips up her t-shirt, grinning. She has the same squishy little Buddha belly she's always had, but now there is a sparkling blue jewel nestled in the centre of it.

"Holy shit."

"Do you like it?"

At this exact moment, the oven timer goes off and saves me from answering, because Angie is more interested in cake than anyone's opinion. Martine takes her golden-brown creation out of the oven, sticks a fork in it to test it, and announces that it's ready. We don't bother icing it. Instead, we cut fat wedges of cake and spread them with Nutella. As we sit at the table eating, I have a sudden vision of the three of us as middle-aged women.

"Hey, is it just me," I say, licking Nutella off my fingers, "Or does time move really fast sometimes?"

"Tell me about it," says Angie. "I swear we were thirteen, like, five minutes ago."

After the long, drawn-out summer, things are moving very quickly now. There are UCAS applications and meetings with the Careers Adviser and a slow surge of panic about A levels. At least I have a vague idea of what I want to do.

"Okay, let's move on to skills and strengths," says Miss Cresswell, flipping the page of a booklet entitled "Planning for My Future."

Miss Cresswell's lipstick and nail polish are the exact same shade of pink, and her hair is done up in one of those very tight buns that you see on ballerinas, women in the military, and cartoon librarians. She looks young – definitely under thirty. I wonder if she likes being a Careers Adviser, or if she's got big plans for what she'll do when she grows up. Maybe when she's not meeting with students she daydreams about becoming a ballerina, or joining the army, or being a librarian. That would explain the hair.

"What springs to mind?" she prompts, and I force myself to focus on the task in hand.

"Um … I'm analytical. Good at … analysing stuff."

"Anything else?"

"I'm good at seeing things from different points of view. Oh, and I have good computer skills, and I'm discreet."

"Discreet?"

"Yeah. That's got to count for something, doesn't it? Like if you're a PA or you go into politics or something."

"Do you want to go into politics?"

"No, I don't like being hated."

The corner of her mouth twitches as she scribbles her notes on the booklet. "Do you have any work experience?"

"This summer I sorted a ton of nuts and bolts – I mean literally a ton – into their different sizes and screwed them all together."

Miss Cresswell writes down 'Perseverance' in the Skills and Strengths section.

"Though technically it was only half a ton because I was working with someone else."

She writes down, 'Teamwork.' "So, you're planning on studying Anthropology," she says, looking up at me with a questioning eyebrow.

"Yep."

"What made you choose that subject?"

"Well, lots of anthropology courses let you study

abroad for a year, which is cool. But mostly I chose it because people are interesting, and I want to understand them. All of them."

Miss Cresswell writes down, 'Ambitious' in the Skills and Strengths section.

diamond

chapter twenty-three

Lana stayed near the entrance of the bar for a while, watching Ralph talking animatedly to a member of the jazz band. The guy was handsome, apart from those ears that stuck out like trophy handles, and his smile was so open and telling that Lana found herself getting a little worried for the two of them. She hadn't worried about anyone else in a long time.

When the guy went to take his place on stage, Lana sidled over to the small table where Ralph was sitting, and took a seat. Ralph's face lit up like the fourth of July.

"Lana! I honestly thought you were dead this time."

"Me too, darling."

They embraced for longer than could be considered decent – Lana reasoned this could only be a good thing if Ralph and his big-eared musician wanted to avoid suspicion

– and then Ralph called the waitress over to them.

"A gimlet for the lady, please," he said, before turning back to Lana. "So, what's new?"

"I don't know where to start. A few scars, I suppose. And this, of course."

Lana placed a hand on the table. The diamond ring caught what little light there was in the bar and threw it back out in all directions. Ralph's eyes went wide and he took Lana's hand, examining the ring with wonder, but also a keen eye for the price of things.

"Holy hell, Lana. Somebody finally made an honest woman outta ya?"

Lana laughed a very unladylike laugh. "Never. I bought it myself. Managed to earn a little money in Germany, though things didn't go so well at first."

"So you're married to the job then."

"You could say that."

"All right. Tell me everything and don't leave anything out, even the shocking stuff. Especially the shocking stuff."

"Not until I've got a few drinks in me. Let's just watch the band for a little while."

bonfire

It's a Saturday evening in November. The sky is just beginning to darken and the air is crisp as a dry leaf. Me,

Ethan, Dad and Darren (who has come home from uni for the weekend) have lit the bonfire at the bottom of the garden, after conscientiously checking it for hedgehogs. It's mostly just dead leaves burning, so it doesn't smell great, but the sight and the sound of it has all four of us slightly hypnotised.

Nobody has said more than two words for a good few minutes. Ethan has been yakking my ear off all afternoon about this girl he met at a LARP thingy. He showed me a picture of her dressed as a goblin and she is cute as a button, even while covered in green face paint. Dad and Darren were chatty as well, when they came out to help get the bonfire started (not that we needed help, but whatever). Dad was full of questions about Darren's second year courses, but Darren was more interested in slagging off his new landlord. Now, though, everyone stares at the flames and says nothing. Sparks fly up, into the deepening darkness, and I feel very calm but in a shivery, tingly way.

"Come on," says Dad quietly, nudging Darren's elbow with his own. "Let's go and help your mum with dinner."

"You two are suspiciously helpful today," I call after them as they trudge back up towards the house. Darren half-turns, then shrugs and grins at me. I shrug and grin back at him. Dad is laboring under a misapprehension regarding me and Ethan, and thinks we will appreciate some alone time in front of a crackling fire.

"You staying for dinner? Mum's making the world's

biggest lasagne."

"Sounds good." Another minute of silence as we get lost watching the fire again. Then, "I'm glad we're still hanging out."

"Why wouldn't we be?"

"I dunno, now that you've got Martine and Angie back, I just thought maybe…"

"I'd replace you? Don't be a twat." I'm actually a little bit flattered at his insecurity about losing me, but then a horrible thought pops up. "You're not going to replace me, are you? If you start going out with goblin girl?"

He laughs, says no, and tells me not to be an idiot. But this train of thought is now running off the rails. "She won't like me. She won't get it; she'll think I'm competition. Just tell her I'm a lesbian, yeah? But don't let her try to fix me up with any girls, I wouldn't know what to do."

"I haven't even asked her out yet! And if she did get jealous of you, I'd just tell her you're like a sister to me."

This gives me a serious case of the warm fuzzies, but I fight them back and plaster a sceptical look on my face. "Am I really, though? You did want to go out with me once."

I'm expecting him to look awkward at that, but instead he looks thoughtful. I let him chew this over, until finally he says, "I suppose you're more like my cousin Dawn."

"What does that mean?"

"We used to play together a lot when we were kids. And then her parents got divorced and her mum took her up to Scotland, so I never saw her for four years. And when they moved back down here, I was fourteen and she was sixteen and... basically she was a knockout."

"Ew, were you actually attracted to her?"

"For, like, one afternoon. It was the shock of seeing her with make-up and... thighs, and things I hadn't noticed before. But then I snapped out of it and she was my cousin Dawn again."

"You realise that's some pretty good blackmail material you've just given me?"

"I've seen you pick your nose with a Q-tip."

"Touché."

Dinner will be nearly ready. I am considering saying something that shouldn't be a big deal. I've said it to Martine and Angie a ton of times. And Mum, and Dad, and even Darren when it's Christmas or he's helped me with an impossible algebra problem or something. But maybe Ethan won't want to hear it. Straight guys don't say it to each other much, and maybe I'm supposed to be playing by their rules. I'm over-analysing. Shut up, brain.

"I love you. As a friend, obviously. And I don't know why I'm even saying it; you don't have to say it back if it's too mushy. Only, I feel like maybe it's important to say these things when you feel them."

"I love you too. And you should always say what you feel."

He says this very decisively. I am a happy bunny.

"I feel hungry."

"I feel like I could eat your mum's lasagne until my stomach literally bursts."

"Darren's probably eaten nothing but Supernoodles since he went back to uni; you'll have to fight him for it."

I feel like I'm right at the beginning of a story, wondering how it will end. Not with a kiss; I know that much.

People put a lot of love into kisses, sometimes, but I don't think I'll ever be able to feel it. They just feel weird and squelchy to me. I'm not bothered, because people put a lot of love into other things, too. Hugs. Lasagne. A shared secret. Forgiveness.

Sometimes, I can feel all the love that's coming my way, flying around my stomach like a cloud of butterflies.

ABOUT THE AUTHOR

Cora Ruskin is a part-time MSc student of Science Communication and works for a charity that helps victims of crime. Writing gets squeezed in between the two. Cora writes fiction and poetry, and blogs at www.corastillwrites.wordpress.com. She lives in Bristol, England, with five housemates and a very messy kitchen. *Other People's Butterflies* is her debut novel.

ACKNOWLEDGMENTS

Firstly, thank you to my brilliant beta readers, Amanda Wood and Rei Odawara. Their insight and advice were so valuable in shaping the story, and their enthusiasm made me feel like it was a story worth telling.

My sincere thanks go to Rose Sinclair, for being unfailingly supportive at every step of the publishing process and for designing the beautiful front cover for *Other People's Butterflies.*

Many thanks are also due to my eagle-eyed editors, Jonathan Lopez and Vicky Cheng. They not only spotted flaws and inconsistencies in the manuscript, but also found unexpected ways of improving it. To everyone at Art Over Chaos – thank you for taking a chance on my story and turning it into a book.

Made in United States
North Haven, CT
28 November 2021

11636354R00113